Is There Rush Hour in a Third World Country?

Rogelio Braga

Translated from Filipino by Kristine Ong Muslim

With an introduction by Eric Abalajon

Published 2022 by the87press

The 87 Press LTD

87 Stonecot Hill

Sutton

Surrey

SM3 9HJ

www.the87press.co.uk

ISBN: 9781739954741

Cover Design by Rayji de Guia

Typesetting: Stanislava Stoilova [www.sdesign.graphics]

Acknowledgments

Grateful acknowledgement is made to the editors of the following publications in which the early version of 'Fungi' first appeared: *Ulirát: Best Contemporary Stories in Translation from the Philippines* (Gaudy Boy, 2021) and *National Translation Month*.

Contents

A Cartography of Desire, Migrations, and Labour:
Introduction by Eric Abalajon

INTRODUCTION: A Cartography of Desire, Migrations, and Labour

Eric Abalajon

This short story collection asks an instinctively answerable question. Of course, there is rush hour in a Third World country. Even before the advent of social media, it is not uncommon to imagine developing countries, via Hollywood for example, through images of traffic-congested cities. Dedicated surveys always place Manila in a notoriously high rank, while other national metropoles like Mexico City or Mumbai are not far behind. Rogelio Braga's stories here were written in the period of 2000-2010, and some came out in major Philippine literary publications. They were collected into a book and published in 2017 by Balangiga Press, an indie press established by Braga themself. The operations of the said indie press have been rocky especially since the start of the Duterte regime in 2016. The tour of Braga's controversial play *Ang Mga Maharlika* (2017), about the affair between former dictator Ferdinand Marcos and actress Dovie Beams, was cancelled because of online harassment and death threats from supporters of the Marcoses and Duterte, made against the people involved in the production. Braga pursued graduate studies in the UK in 2018 and was granted asylum status in 2022. *Is There Rush Hour in a Third World Country?*, now translated into English by Kristine Ong Muslim, offers a glimpse into the lives of people behind a seemingly fixed imaginary—blistering heat, permanent fog of dust and pollution, loud honking of vehicles, motorists and passengers in a spatial and temporal limbo. Braga goes beyond this Third World sensory ordeal, and maps out the intersections of desire and disenchantment, mobility and suspension, between marginalised characters and the built environments where they try to make do or escape.

Amid this urban disorder, it is telling that there is an abundance of stories of romance in the collection. Frequently they depict young adults going through a final coming of age of sorts, trying to find a sense of meaning in the middle of loneliness and job precarity. In 'Ministop', the namesake of a prominent 24-hour convenience store chain, a diligent call centre agent called Jessica takes a break from her routine and starts a friendship with a man who also goes out for his lunch at 3 a.m. The particular branch where they meet provides a refuge from the nocturnal grind. The proliferation of such establishments in Philippine cities coincided with the business processing outsourcing (BPO) boom of the early 2000s. The sector was greeted with optimism for being able to cater to new generations of a well-educated, and specifically English-proficient, surplus labour force with perpetually limited employment options. The two characters discuss the changing city, their views on work, and developments in national politics. Jessica is grateful to the then-President, Gloria Macapagal Arroyo (2001-2010), for facilitating the entry of BPO companies and the opportunities that came along with them. The man, however, intuitively counters: 'Dumami rin ang mga puyat' ('The number of sleepless people also increased'). The blossoming romance is cut short when the man confides that he wants to quit. Jessica, who all the time assumes him to be another agent, casually recognises the high turnover rate of the industry. The man then admits he belongs to an even older sector, where people also roam the streets at night, which existed before the advent of highrise offices. The revelation kills every ounce of Jessica's yearning for emotional connection and pulls her back to seek measurable validation in the industry that aims to make life easier for a clientele in a different time zone. In the story 'Emilio Echeverri', another girl called Betilda takes a more nonchalant outlook on a relationship that fails to take off. For a time she worked

2

for a labour agency processing the papers of seafarers in an office located in the old capital, Intramuros. One night after work, she meets a dashing man on the dancefloor, Emilio. For her and her office friends, he's simply the 'guy from Letran', carrying connotations of being a student from the prestigious university also found in the same section of the city. After observing a mysterious incident involving Emilio during the day, things become tense, and later for Betilda, hazy. Over drinks with former officemates, after being retrenched and relocating to work in another part of the city, she admits the man might as well be a ghost- stories of which are pervasive in the so-called walled city.

The romance mode is brought outside the national capital, the sprawl of which—political, economic, cultural— can be considered to extend into the rest of the country. In 'Ang Karengkeng ng Rural Tours' ('The Flirt of Rural Tours'), a developmental worker simply called 'a Tagalog' to emphasise his outsider status, flirts with another passenger on a long-distance bus travelling between the Southern urban centres Iligan City and Davao City. The man turns out to be a soldier, another outsider in Mindanao, who starts talking about his travels and knowledge of the region. He eventually begins bragging slyly about his number of kills and praising the superficial 'peace and order' established in certain areas. Here, the overlapping culture of violence and machismo is manifested even in mundane encounters, from the conversation among strangers to the formulaic action movie playing on the bus to amuse passengers travelling in the region where an 'all-out war' is being waged. Meanwhile 'Sa Outpost' ('At the Outpost') takes place in Cebu City, where another NGO worker, Tobias, decides to enjoy some downtime from fieldwork. In a bookstore inside a high-end mall, he meets Sissy, who shows him around the pockets of leisure the city can offer. While inside a bar celebrating reggae month, Tobias juxtaposes the present space and moment of gratification to the communities he just left: 'Kung babagsakan ng bomba ang bar, tulad ng bomba na inihulog ng gubyerno ni Arroyo sa North Cotabato ilang buwan na ang nakararaan, iyong bomba na pumatay sa mga batang Maguindanaoan na nasa loob ng kanilang payag, iyong bomba na walang pinipiling lahi, relihiyon, kasarian, at edad—ilang ulit marahil mapapaslang si Bob Marley na tapyas ang mukha o di kaya'y nagkahiwa-hiwalay ang mga bahagi ng katawan.' ('If a bomb was dropped on the bar, like that bomb that the Arroyo government dropped on North Cotabato some months ago, that bomb that killed Maguindanaon children in their huts, that bomb that killed all people regardless of their race, religion, gender, and age—Bob Marley would probably die many deaths, and be defaced or with body parts severed.') As the evening drags on, an unspoken affinity is revealed between the two, in regard to the manifold things they are trying to escape. They give in, achieving a transactional form of intimacy, which in a nation where violence is continuously reproduced and hidden, seems to be as good as it gets. The subject of insurgency in the nation's peripheries is elaborated further in Braga's noirish novel *Colon* (2016), where rival projects of self-determination, the afterlives of trauma, and the rewriting of history are blended.

Braga brings open armed conflict back to the national metropole through the speculative mode in 'Kabanalan sa Panahon ng Digmâ' ('Piety in Wartime'). Two children in the distant future, Imo and Wanda, observe how corpses are collected from the Pasig River after every clash or bombing. The country is again a battleground for competing imperial powers, this time between the 'US Empire' and the 'Beijing Government'. The story recalls World War II narratives of Manila in ruins, considered a defining moment in a generation's loss of innocence, while at the same time anxiously anticipating the possible confrontation building up in the Pacific over the last two decades. As the two friends try to get to the bottom of the mystery, hints can be detected that the plot will fall into the *Soylent Green* trope, but Braga aims for something much more profound. The resolution of past, present, and future conflicts over resources is apparently so obvious, and the folly is failing to recognise it as such. The Pasig River, the capital's main waterway, figures again in 'Fungi,' another mapping of the city from the perspective of children who come to terms with the fact that Manila's striking spatial disparities can be in such close proximity to each other. An informal community beside a dumpsite called Lupang Pangako, literally 'Promised Land' (a moniker also used to describe Mindanao), is where two friends Biring and Buni one day come across a slippery and fragrant object. They immediately declare it to be magical, showing a child's sense of wonder but also a symptom of their dire living conditions. The next day, they head out for an adventure into the city to find the magic's source. They observe, 'Parang araw-araw na nagbibihis ang lungsod: laging bago at di nakabuburyong. Minamasdan nila ang mga nagtatayugang gusali, ang mabibilis na sasakyan, ang mga batang may bitbit na bag at papasok sa eskuwela, ang mga kotse, ang mga sakay ng kotse. Tila isa itong bagong mundo para sa kanila. Ito ang mundo ng mahika, ito ang pinanggalingan ng bagay na kanilang hinahanap.' ('As for the city, it kept changing what it wore daily: its outfits were always new and never boring. [They] did not tire from observing the tall buildings, the vehicles that hurtled past them, the schoolbag-toting children on their way to school, the cars, the people inside the cars. All these seemed like an entirely different world to them. This was the world of enchantment. This was the one true source of the magical thing they were looking for.') A crucial moment is when the friends enter a shopping mall and see display shelves filled with consumer goods, objects which they only know through their plastic packaging. A security guard catches a whiff of them, literally, and bars them from entering again. The poor can only experience the city through its refuse, or indeed by constituting the city's refuse themselves. The mall is contrasted with a story they were told, of a Mutya, loosely translatable as 'enchantress', supposedly residing in the river, one that doesn't discriminate and welcomes everyone who wishes to seek shelter.

If one is looking for some semblance of a hopeful closure, this is hard-won and found in the stories 'Sinta' ('Beloved') and 'Lahat ng Linggong Tahimik' ('All the Quiet Sundays'). Both stories involve lower middle-class families, where children take on the struggle for upward mobility initiated by their parents, with whom they have ambivalent relationships. 'Beloved' is presented as the long sermon of an older sibling who inherited a parental role and is furious at his youngest sibling, an indolent teenager. The plea for help with chores inside the house is revealed to be a form of displacement to prevent vicious cycles from continuing. The eldest brother narrates how their father went to Iraq as a construction work even amid the Gulf War, just for him to be able to enrol in a private school and presumably have better employment options. Things didn't work out abroad, and the patriarch returned home sick and depressed. This, in turn, provoked episodes of alcoholism and domestic violence before his passing. Still, fond memories are shared, like how as children they watched a coup d'état staged by soldiers against President Cory Aquino (1986-1992) unfold in the capital's highways, much to the anger of their worried mother. Power struggles, then and now, tend to be mere spectacle for the disempowered. The overlapping of violence cultivated in the community, the city, the country, and the world has found its way into their home. The least they can do is keep it clean. Closure is also what is being aspired to in 'All the Quiet Sundays', a parallel story about another problematic father, Porboy. Like many men of his generation and class, he worked in the Middle East for a time, then undergoing an oil boom. He has already departed but still haunts the wife and son who survive him. The story begins with the news of a friend and coworker of his, Ninong Andy, about to visit their home. Preparations made by the mother and son bring back memories of the routine of dealing with the aftermath of receiving guests. This entails 'pagliligpit ng mga platito ng mani, mga plastik ng chicharon, mga bote ng alak, paglalampaso sa mga súka ng mga lasing, dura, basa mula sa mga natapong alak at tubig at piraso ng yelong tumalsik sa sahig, sa maayos na pagsasalansan ng mga nakabalandrang katawang bumagsak na sa sala sa kalasingan. Ito ang Lunes ng madaling-araw sa bahay namin o ang Linggo ng hapon kung sakaling maagang babagsak sa kalasingan si Porboy at ang mga kasama niya sa inuman' ('[...] clearing the platters heaped with peanuts, the ripped plastic containers of chicharon, and the beer bottles, the mopping up of vomit, spit, beer spills and ice bucket splashes, to the careful rearrangement of the passed-out bodies of intoxicated men. All this took up the wee hours of Monday mornings or Sunday afternoons'). The story is notable as it also narrates the experience of leaving the provinces before migrating to Manila; Porboy is from Negros, and his wife, tagged as 'Waray', is presumably from Eastern Visayas. It is as if the varied geography of the archipelago comprises stopovers in the pursuit of trying to get by, each stage filled with tension and sacrifices, and each departure or homecoming equally distressful.

As is apparent by now, the burden of economic class is a recurring theme in all of Braga's stories, but it is most concentrated in 'Bona Bien' as well as the title story. Soledad is a fresh graduate who started working in an insurance company in the middle of a strike. Aside from the labour disruption, she also encounters office microaggressions like gossip and just plain difficulty in collaboration. A lot of the animosity comes from an older employee, Bona, who Soledad later cosies up to after seeing her unexpectedly outside of work. During weekends, they share stories about their respective careers and relationships, especially horrible experiences with the men in their lives. Their occasional rants draw direct parallels with the scandalous short-term of President Erap Estrada (1998-2001), the former action star turned politician, a notorious womaniser who was later deposed for embezzlement charges. Despite better relations with the likes of Bona, Soledad often finds herself in a thorny position in the workplace. At the onset, she is groomed to think she is part of the 'management side', which she readily embraces at first due to the cultural capital she has accrued in possessing a degree from a top university. Looking into the fine print of her contract, however, reveals her to be equally precarious. When an even bigger crisis looms in the company, she is fed with more deceptive corporate terms like 'voluntary retirement' and 'business process re-engineering', and made to scorn older employees such as Bona as they are becoming 'redundant'. Friendship is exposed as a futile buffer against the flooding of foreign capital and the weakening of trade unions, and not everyone survives the crisis in the now-ironically named All Filipino Life Insurance Corporation. Upon the offer of a promotion in the newly restructured company, Soledad experiences 'deadlock', the managerial concept now penetrating her life beyond her job title. She rushes to a mall, enters a movie theater, and distracts herself from her dilemma, at least temporarily. 'May Rush Hour Ba Sa Third World?' ('Is There Rush Hour in a Third World Country?') has the making of, and does start off as, a quirky misadventure. Two domestic helpers, Elsa and Choning, use their once-a-week day off to traverse the streets of Manila as one of them agrees to meet up with a textmate, an updated form of pen pal. Their excitement and giddiness about the meeting and where it could lead to are repeatedly broken down by various incidents on the brutal commute; harassment or rudeness from other passengers and the bus conductor, or witnessing physical and emotional strain inflicted on others. Their migratory background is revealed right away in exchanges like 'Hindi naman ganito sa atin. Ako na ang nagsabi sa iyo na ganito talaga rito sa Maynila' ('It wasn't like this back home. I told you this is how it is in Manila'), and '...ganyan talaga ang buhay dito sa Maynila' ('[...] this is really how it is in Manila'). The cruelty of the capital is an ordeal, but it must be endured. As women in their twenties, a romance and possible marriage is seen as a disruptor of their daily grind. In the long commute, they recollect stories of others in their line of work, again revealing the stages of labour migration. The anecdotes of those acquaintances who also left the provinces for Manila are recounted, one eventually daring to work in a place like Macau, a nearby tiger economy city with a high demand for cheap domestic helpers, before finally arriving, through a stroke of luck, in the ultimate spatial signpost of success: the United States. These iterations of the Cinderella story, where fortitude and chance dominate, keep their spirits up, as the slow pace of cars parallels their aspirations for love and class mobility. Their exhaustion is relieved when they finally arrive in Quiapo Church, the meetup place as a shelter for the faithful and the apprehensive. They wait for the man beside the Black Nazarene, whose devotees are known to have the power to bring the city to a standstill, in a very different manner from the pilgrimage they just survived.

The power of Braga's work is always a question of narrative position, of whose stories are being told. This collection does not include that other type of tale concerning the tormented local (actually transnational) bourgeois, lamenting the sorry state of their country. These stories tend to be presented in polished formalism, a packaging presumed to be most palatable to Anglophone audiences, and almost always convey a safe and detached liberalism of inaction. The conflicts Braga outlines might suggest an ethos of defeat or hopelessness, but slippage into these positions is prevented by the dignified perseverance of their characters, framed by the storyteller's sharp attention to the details of respective and overlapping habitus. Poverty and violence are depicted with nuance and never intended to elicit pity or indulgently generate spectacle. When moral crossroads are encountered, often at the end, one is provoked to think outward into the histories and the mappings of places, lives, and relations. These predicaments—of the urban poor, of young workers, of fractured nuclear families, of people in regions with armed conflict—are not innate and don't come out of nowhere. They are exercises in substantiating agency in a postcolonial country, and the identities always emerge as intersectional by default. Here, picking one struggle at a time is a luxury very few can afford. Class, gender, locality, and nationhood are interrogated in the backdrop of institutionalised low-intensity conflict, labour-export, cultural imperialism, and structural adjustments. There are no elites, or caricatures of them, in these stories where we can direct our rightful rage. Instead, we encounter classes of people in the lowest rung of society mistreating each other primarily due to the personal shortsightedness brought about by the demand for survival. This is a testament to the need for comprehensive and systemic change, and forms of inward retreat into happiness and contentment will definitely stand on shaky foundations. The deliberate use of 'Third World' instead of 'Developing' to describe a country is a declaration that it is not a question of catching up in order to taste the elusive fruits of neoliberalism, but a demand to reimagine better living conditions for people who can barely take a break from labour or know very little of life outside of it. The interregnum that is Braga's fiction is not a mediation on the Philippines alone, but for all peoples trying to break away from deadlocks in one form or another, who may hopefully be reached by this translation.

Bona Bien

Deadlock. This was the first word I learnt from the corporate world and the one word whose meaning I grasped without question. I also intuitively understood the various ways it could be used for describing experiences, for describing life. No wonder, because on my first day at work and after spending four years in college, a strike was the first thing the so-called corporate world gave me a taste of. On my first day at All Filipino Life Insurance Corporation, I was greeted by the sight of employees on strike. The union and company management could not agree on a salary increase for the rank-and-file and better benefits for midyear and Christmas, as well as yearly increase bonuses.

"Don't mind them. You can't join the union since you're on the management side." This was the second lesson I got from the corporate world: if you were not union, you were management, and vice versa. I remembered this particular lesson from Ms. Dahlen, the company's HRD manager. It was hard to stop watching the mole dancing on her cheek, which made her appear as if she was always frowning at people. Her mole had its own distinctive movements: left-to-right during casual conversations. It was also pretty obvious when she was lying, what with her mole's up-down motion, especially when she was talking about the union.

"Ay sus! Stop already. That drama is so college level," Bona said when I told her how much I wanted to work for famous TV stations, to the point of reaching Singapore and becoming an MTV VJ or a popular newscaster.

"Hay naku, Bona, you have no idea. Besides, there's that generation gap," I said. "You don't watch MTV. I'm sure you only watch *Meteor Garden* or *Mari Mar*!"

"Know what, it's really puzzling that kids nowadays

take courses in college. Like you, for example. Mass Comm. With the number of students taking that up, there might not be enough TV jobs for all of you!"

"That's harsh. I'm a UP Diliman graduate, anyway. Just look at our president- once an actor, on TV, loved by the masses... popular."

"If I can go back, I will take up nursing. In other countries, there's a demand for nurses these days. That can even be my ticket to America. I will have my Michelle take up nursing." Bona had a twelve-year-old daughter named Michelle, who would have been in high school now if she hadn't been forced to stop Grade Three because of kidney disease and the need for dialysis treatment twice a month.

"But why? I can still get to others. I worked so hard in UP, a cum laude," I kept telling Bona jokingly. "My qualifications are international."

"Ay! Good luck with your career. I'll never get you, Soledad, your idealism that belongs to the yesteryear era of Rizal. Degrees are no longer needed – because our times demand street smarts – skills! Skills! Like what Dahlen says. Look at me, a college graduate and already working so hard. And yet I still have sidelines like selling tocino, longganisa, hotdogs, Avon, SO-EN, even Forever Living products just so I can pay for my daughter's needs. I can't understand why God seems to be putting all of my punishments into my child. Good for Erap for committing to serve the poor, but your diploma can't even be used to settle your MERALCO bills."

Bona and I were in the same department, Policy Services. Our job included answering policy holders' questions, processing claims, and monitoring the contract effectiveness of annual, semi-annual, quarterly, or monthly premiums. My rank was Policy Services Assistant Level I ('But that's supervisory level, hija,' Ms. Dahlen would say), while Bona, who had been working in the company far longer than me, had a Level V rank ('Rank and file… unlike you from UP' was the gist of the gossip shared to me by Ms. Dahlen's staffer at HRD). Since my first few months at work, Bona was already cold towards me. I simply chalked it up to the then-concluded strike, the hangover from her days and nights on the picket line. But it got worse later, as she was outright rude to me whenever I made errors in encoding policy numbers. She gave me hell during my first six months at the company.

"Here in the corporate world, everything is corporate. Corporate attire, corporate gestures and manner of speaking. And most of all, corporate coffee. Everything here is a property of the corporation. So, if you can help yourself, don't just get coffee from the coffeemaker because I make that every morning for Boss Tsip." This was how Bona berated me when she saw me pouring coffee from our department manager's coffeemaker.

I first attributed her rudeness to envy. Bona had been with the company for almost 20 years, and yet the only raise she ever got involved her salary and plucked eyebrows. As for me, I just got hired, a fresh graduate yet already a supervisor. But after seeing her pay grade which increased yearly because of their union CBA, I realised I was wrong in thinking she was envious of my measly pay. My rank was supervisor, but my salary was intended for the rank-and-file. It was also 'supervisory,' so I could not join the union.

Every day at the office was hell. There was the endless clatter of punchers, staplers, tape dispensers, as well as our constant snide remarks to each other, remarks that were filled with bitterness and resentment. In the beginning, I didn't intend to talk back to someone older than me, plus I didn't think I had anything to gain from picking a fight with someone who didn't even finish school at UP. I even considered resigning because of the hostile environment where you had to work with someone you despised with all your heart. Ultimately, I realised resigning was like letting the gaga win. I thought I should give Bona hell and make it hard for her to make me quit my job.

I also could not make sense of the attitude of long-time workers in the company. I heard new rumours about myself practically every day, rumours about me supposedly not being a virgin anymore because I was from UP, that I was a kiss-ass, a know-it-all even if I was very new to the company and still had so much to learn, and about all sorts of things ranging from what shoes I wore to what I had in my packed lunch. Mama said that was really how it was for new hires. The old-timers in the company would pick on you. In Magnolia Ice Cream-speak, you were the 'Flavour of the Month.' But Mama told me not to be demoralised, that I should let the experience toughen me up as she had undergone the exact same treatment from the company where she retired after almost 40 years. It was the same company where she met Papa. My godparents were also their office mates. That's just how it is, Mama said, in the 'real world', where you have to earn and you have the constant need to earn so there's no choice but to endure it and find a way to get along with your coworkers.

"Just don't mind their insecurities," said Ms. Dahlen, the mole moving up and down her left cheek. "You have to understand that many of them are unionised. Look at our union members: all they know is how to leech off money from the company. Some of them haven't even graduated from college and only got hired because Human Resources and Development was not a thing 20 years ago."

At some point, all of them got tired of targeting me and diverted their attention to that new hire at the Accounting Division. Bona's ill-treatment of me, however, did not change. There were times I thought about confronting her. I just could not muster enough courage to do it. She always looked like she was geared up for a fight. Scary. Thick makeup, bright red lips, high heels, and, most of all, that mouth that lashed out at anyone. This image of Bona was how I saw her back then. That's our tendency—we judge people who we don't know according to our own self-imposed standards. I didn't know Bona very well at that time.

How Bona and I made peace is a memory which will stay with me for as long as I live and as long as her memory remains in my heart. It was Saturday, and there was no office work when I rushed to see my third, and probably last, La Salle boyfriend, who was doing his OJT at the accounting department of a dialysis centre on Aurora Boulevard. I could no longer remember his name, though I was sure he was the nephew of the dialysis centre owner. How we met: during a rare instance when I went to a Starbucks in Vito Cruz, he approached me with an offer of a Frappuccino and his name. After a long conversation, the topics of which ranged from the Eraserheads concert to the annoyance he felt towards Erap, we clicked and were 'together' that same night. Amazing how our desire for each other grew cold fast like the coffees in Starbucks. I'd been meaning to end our relationship, which lasted for more than three semesters of him trying to complete his back-subjects at the De La Salle University, when I heard about his addiction to ecstasy. I was under the impression he was over his drug abuse problems. I threatened him with a breakup if he kept using anything that was not 'natural'. Then I heard about that gago flirting with a woman at Friendster. Erap and him were much too alike, a drunkard, a womaniser.

The smell stopped me when I got near the centre's foyer. The strong pungent odour of the dialysis centre felt like it had barbs latching inside my nose. *Shit, I don't think I can take the smell of this place*, I said to myself. There were several sofas in the centre and dextrose packets were strung up like ornaments. I looked around for that asshole. The walls were all painted white. On top of that was the chill from all five air conditioning units. Three television sets were set up for the patients' visitors and carers because dialysis treatment took up almost half a day. It was obvious which patients had no kin or friends accompanying them during their treatment. I also noticed the ease with which dialysis was performed: the patient simply reclined on the sofa or lay down in the bed, then the process of removing waste from their body ensued.

I asked the front desk assistant whether my boyfriend was on duty. Luckily, he wasn't. The necessary task of ending another relationship was weighing me down so I slumped on the sofa, crying. I tried to disguise my sobs by pretending I was simply yawning with one hand covering my mouth. Of course it was embarrassing to be bawling my eyes out and have people take me for an emo girl reenacting an MTV video with the Backstreet Boys's 'I'll Never Break Your Heart' in the background.

"Hey, bruha, stop that drama," said a voice behind me, before there was a pat on my shoulder.

"Bona?" I could not believe that in this place I was seeing the one reason it was hard for me to get to the office every morning. "Bona Bien, is that you?"

"Maybe."

It really surprised me to see this side of Bona. Maybe she was really like this outside of work.

Bona invited me to join her in the part of the centre where her daughter was receiving treatment. "That's where my kid is getting her dialysis. Let's go over there, talk for a while. I saw you when you came in. So, what's with that drama of yours?"

I had no stomach for rehashing what was up with me and my boyfriend, let alone for opening up about it to no one other than Bona, the great nagger and tattletale, so that by Monday the entire office would have heard about my love life. But Bona won my trust when I met her daughter. It wasn't so much Bona herself who secured my trust, but the pity I felt for her daughter.

"Here, Michelle, you have a visitor."

"Good morning," she said, lying on the sofa. In her navel were all sorts of tubes where blood, medicine, and bodily toxins flowed.

"Say hello to Tita Soly."

I smiled and waved at her, secretly surveying all the tubes stuck to her body.

"Don't worry, Tita Soly, none of that hurts," Michelle said, noticing where I was looking.

Bona motioned for me to sit next to her as she tidied up the empty containers for McDonald's hamburgers and french fries which Michelle ate. She explained that dialysis was like that, that the patient had to be fed first with what she was not supposed to eat. The treatment process would eliminate the newly introduced toxins, anyway. Still, in the days before and after the treatment, salty and fatty foods were prohibited. The kidneys were for cleaning the blood circulating in the body. Kidney failure would ultimately result in septic shock, and that's where dialysis came in. The dialysis machine and the tubes connected to Michelle were standins for urination to eliminate the toxins filtered from the body by the kidneys. Both of Michelle's kidneys were gone, so her continued survival was dependent on dialysis.

"I know why you're crying."

At first I did not reply to Bona, but after her soothing shoulder massage to calm me down, I cried on her shoulders and told her everything.

"Ay sus! Stop crying!"

I was helpless to stop. Michelle busied herself watching her favorite MTV Artist of the Month, the Backstreet Boys. I told Bona all about my boyfriend. She listened to me in earnest, and I could see she was sincere in her sympathy.

"That's just life, Soly. Look at me, a failure. I split with Michelle's father after I found out that he had been shacking up with another woman in America. The bastard initially went to Saudi to work. After eight months, he stopped writing, stopped sending money. It was already too late when I heard he was living with someone else and that they went to America. His dick probably went itchy from the Saudi heat and couldn't resist that nurse, a Filipina. Shame she had no conscience," said Bona, her voice and manner of speaking exuding strength. "Oh well, just like Erap and all his women." This had both of us giggling.

"Why didn't you fight? You could have sued."

"I'm just a humble employee," she said, grinning at her mention of 'humble employee'. "Back when CBA wasn't a thing, I could only draw the minimum wage. I did think many times about suing him, getting the remittances I was entitled to, but I just couldn't stand the mess of that as well as the expenses for a lawyer's fee. The agency that sent him to Saudi couldn't do anything, either, because he immediately flew to the United States, plus Michelle needed close attention." I was sure what Bona meant by 'attention' was the 15,000 pesos needed every two weeks for Michelle's dialysis treatment.

I could see Bona was uncomfortable talking about this in front of her daughter. It was noon, and there were five more hours before Michelle could be discharged. We continued our chat at the reception area, munching on watermelon seeds.

"That's just human life, Soly. We meet someone and then part ways with that person later."

Initially, I found it hard to trust Bona given our history at the office. I was not used to seeing this side of her. Although it was interesting to hear her talk about serious issues, her tone was like the one she used when spreading gossip.

"Maybe the time has come for me to stop believing in relationships."

"You're too young, Soly, to have that kind of outlook."

"I've even lost my faith in marriage. Marriage is just an economic arrangement, right?"

"You're really from UP. That's how people from that school think even during our time, even during Martial Law. They needlessly complicate things which don't merit time and energy, things that are not necessary in our lives."

"Ay! Why be specific and involve the school?"

"That's exactly how I thought when I was your age. Remember, Soly, once you've experienced earning money and realise its role in your survival, your views will change."

More patients continued to enter the dialysis centre. Some moved with the aid of their wheelchairs, clutching dextrose strands with tubes attached to their bodies through their navels. There were kids, old people, people my age. I got distracted sometimes and kept glancing at them while listening to Bona.

"So, what was your previous belief? Were you a hippie? Existentialist? Atheist? Or communist?"

"Gaga, there's nothing like that at Lyceum."

I was excited to hear Bona talk about these things, to discover the two of us having common beliefs.

"Have you heard of the Philosophy of Two?"

"What? No, not yet. Who's behind that?"

"Of course you haven't heard of it. I invented it." Bona laughed as if she were making fun of me again. "I believe all things are created in pairs. See, I'm the only one who knows that? God made things in pairs. There's heaven and earth, good and evil, woman and man, husband and wife, hot and cold. Your body, all too symmetrical from head to toe: your eyes, nose, lungs, kidneys, feet, hands. So there, that's my philosophy." Bona had many things to say about her philosophy. She even said it began with her name. "Good thing our annulment was quickly approved."

"Really?"

"Because I could have been Mrs. Bona Busoy until now! I had to take a loan for that annulment."

"You're right, terrible name. What a bad combination."

Many Saturdays after that encounter I became a regular visitor to the dialysis centre. Bona and I would chat all day as if the two of us were not in the same office during weekdays. And because Michelle could be safely left alone at the dialysis centre, Bona and I would end up spending time at Megamall to watch movies or do window shopping, which was how I discovered Bona's attraction to Louis Vuitton bags. Both of us couldn't afford the latter. We just loved looking at the bags. I also learned of her love for Hollywood films. We had work-related discussions, too.

"That's what I would not exchange for anything else, my job at All Filipino Life Insurance Corporation. There were moments when I tried to leave and resign. There was a time when my salary was like the equivalent of pocket change. It only improved because of the union and CBA. So I figure if I resign now, no company will hire me considering my age. Competition is also tight as there are many graduates every year. Some of them even have a hard time finding a job. Hay! Why is it that I'm only thinking of resigning now that I'm old." Then Bona would inhale deeply as she reflected on the precarity of her career path.

Bona and I stayed on good terms since then. In the office, we continued with the small talk, plus I also learned from her how to sell panties, Avon, tocino, longganisa, as well as take on all sorts of gigs. My La Salle boyfriend? Vanished without a trace. Bona heard that he had asked for a transfer to another branch as soon as I became a regular visitor to the centre. I promised myself I would never ever fall for a man who would offer a Frappuccino with his name at a Starbucks, a name I would end up forgetting after all.

"Michelle should have been in high school by now. She was Grade Three when she first complained about pain in her midsection. At first I thought it was just a UTI, so we didn't seek treatment early, just gave her water and buko juice. Then Michelle rushed home early from school one day and said her waist area was painful. That night her whole body became swollen." Bona paused from her recollection. This was during one of those Saturdays we spent together at the reception area. Bona cried, my first time seeing her cry. She was not that strong, or brash, like how I used to see her in the office.

"Michelle has been on dialysis for almost three years now. I feel sorry for my child. Ay sus, I'm crying again..." Bona talked about the days when Michelle's body would swell from the waist down, and how one morning she screamed nonstop after waking up with watery discharges soaking her thighs. Bona described how she softly sobbed as she wiped the water coming out of Michelle, the water seeping down the mattress, and how she had never made her pity obvious in the presence of her daughter. "Dialysis keeps Michelle alive. If I miss one Saturday session, it could have serious consequences, like toxins in her body reaching her brain."

A visit to the dialysis centre cost them in excess of 15,000 pesos, a sum that already covered the cost of the medicine, fees for the centre, and blood. I wondered how Bona was able to produce such an amount as a rank-and-file worker.

"Some days I can't get out of my head the hopelessness and stress of having to cough up money each time to pay the bills, so I make plans to sell a body part. There is nothing else for me to sell," said Bona, jokingly, one time when I asked her about it.

The employees had a meeting one day. The union called for it. Union meetings were always held during lunch breaks, so I ended up eating alone in the pantry as Bona attended what she said was a very important meeting. After the meeting, she returned to her office table, looking shaken and disturbed. I was desperate for news but was too scared to ask lest I got viewed as a snitch on behalf of the management by the department where I belonged. Thankfully, Bona told me what the meeting was about.

"Soly, leche, looks like there will be another strike."

"Why? Is the union going to demand an increase in wages and benefits again?"

"It's worse," she said, taking a deep breath as if siphoning strength from her very soul. "There will be more firings."

I was shocked. And scared, but not for myself because I knew I could always get hired elsewhere and was confident about better opportunities outside All Filipino Life Insurance Corporation. Bona was the only thing keeping me here. I was worried about her losing her job and what that would do to Michelle's dialysis treatment. I spent sleepless nights agonising about Bona and her family.

It was noon when I went to see Ms. Dahlen in her office.

"Now where on earth did you hear that?" Ms. Dahlen said, startled by my question. "Those union members are really making me angry. I guess you heard that from Bona. I can see the two of you are getting cosy with each other. Hay! You getting mixed up with them is not a good look. Those union members grew up in an old system." There was derisiveness in her tone whenever she said 'those union members'.

"Old system?"

"What else do you expect? It's as if they're working for the Philippine government. All right, I admit, Soly, there will be another round of firings."

Hearing Ms. Dahlen's admission was a shock to me. But what I found most disturbing was her nonchalance, like it never occurred to her that actual people were involved and set to lose their jobs, and one of them could be Bona Bien.

"You have nothing to worry about. The ones who will be fired are the older employees whose skills haven't been upgraded. They deserve to be put in voluntary retirement."

"But why do we need to fire people?"

"Simple. The company can no longer afford to pay useless rank-and-file employees who are not productive all the time. Some of them have tasks which overlap. Just like you and Bona. You can do it alone. MS Department can create programs to automate the processes and all of Bona's tasks."

I knew Bona would be fired.

Ms. Dahlen settled on her soft backrest and placed her hands on her table. Its surface shone like a mirror. She gently explained: "The company is losing money, Soly. Many foreign companies are entering the country. Competition within the industry is becoming way too tight. We need competitive individuals like you." And because Ms. Dahlen had a habit of appeasing me, she said: "And this is confidential information. That's one of the benefits when you're part of management: access to confidential matters."

And Ms. Dahlen's words became flesh, so to speak. The company fired people en masse, and one of them was Bona. There was mayhem during the week of the strike. For one, the NLRC declared the strike illegal. Our office operations had to be transferred somewhere else. There was a clash between the police and some of the striking workers because it was claimed that the workers pelted the office's glass windows with stones. Union officials went on a hunger strike. In the end, the management prevailed. The company claimed it did not have the budget to maintain a large number of employees on its payroll; a layoff was not only deemed the most effective solution to the problem, it was also somehow hailed as a move that was fair to both the management and the union. 'Business process re-engineering' was what Ms. Dahlen called it. A smooth, fancy term. One could almost believe its truthfulness, as truthful as Erap's propaganda on TV. She said that I should think of the poor policy holders in the event of the company going bankrupt and closing down. Some workers, faced with no other choice, agreed to a 'voluntary retirement.' A few of them, as they were on probationary status or contractuals, did not even get a single peso after being booted out of the company. Bona, according to the union president, got retirement benefits after the retrenchment.

I did not see Bona after that. Week after week, I kept showing up at the dialysis centre with the hope that I would see her again. I was really scared for Michelle. Was she still having her treatments, or could they no longer afford to keep making the weekly trips to the centre? I realised how much Bona's friendship meant to me, how important she was as a colleague and as a friend. Shame how sometimes we only saw a coworker's worth as a person in her absence, once she has resigned, her contract lapsed as a casual, or she's been fired after a retrenchment.

Because Bona had been with the few 'survivors' of the layoff for a long time, I was able to get pieces of information about her whereabouts. Someone from the MIS Department gave me Bona's home address. I did not wait for the week to end before finding Bona. I applied for vacation leave on Friday. The address given to me indicated an area somewhere on Commonwealth Avenue in Quezon City. The area was difficult to get to. I rode two tricycles and then walked a few corner intersections, asking locals along the way. I didn't know what came over me that day but I felt desperate to find Bona.

When I finally reached the street corner stated in the address, I approached a banana-cue vendor for directions to Bona's house. I remembered Bona telling me before that in the event I find myself in her area, I should not be surprised by her reputation as 'Bona, who separated from her husband'. The place was disorderly and crowded. Kids were running down the streets. Jeepneys were parked at the side of roads. Loiterers were all over the place, like pieces of trash waiting for whoever would care to pick them up for loading into a garbage truck. The street corner in Bona's area had been laid with asphalt. There were concrete houses as well as dilapidated shacks.

"Soly?" a voice behind me sounded.

"Oy, Bona!" It was almost impossible to speak from the overwhelming feeling of joy and relief of seeing her again. "I had a hard time finding your house; thankfully your beauty is here in the flesh."

"Here, let's go inside," Bona said, leading me inside her house which was not as big as her neighbours', but was at least made of concrete and had new corrugated metal roofing.

"How's Michelle? Haven't seen her for four months."

Bona smiled and said Michelle was already in America: her father took her to get treated and hopefully arrange for a kidney transplant. This news gave me so much joy. "Naku, she'll probably be back by next month. I don't know, I'm sure she'll be back."

"Good thing you let him take Michelle."

Bona never broached the topic again and instead talked about her new business. She said she was earning more now, more than her previous salary in our company. I ended our conversation by giving her updates on her now-former coworkers.

In the months that followed, Bona and I continued our Saturday get-togethers: watching movies, chatting, doing leisure walks. Sometimes I asked how Michelle was doing and all she would say was "she's okay" and then immediately change the topic. We rarely talked about Michelle.

It was noon while we were shopping for cloth fabric in Ylaya in Divisoria when Bona collapsed and lost consciousness. I thought it was probably due to the suffocatingly hot weather, though it really terrified me seeing Bona turning deathly pale, her face swollen. I managed to get her into a taxi and took her to her house. She slowly recovered once we were there, telling me she was going to be alright and that I should leave. I was worried about her and asked to stay with her for a while, but she almost begged for me to leave. So I did, carrying my shopping bags.

The next time I visited her was on my birthday, which was not the reason I came to see her. I had good news to share. "Hay! Bona, guess what?" I greeted her as soon as she opened the door. Her appearance floored me. She looked like another person, with deep-set eyes and an emaciated body. She wore a duster dress, and her hand cradled the area around her navel where something seemed to protrude. I learned later how that part of her body had swollen up badly. "What happened to you?"

Bona did not immediately answer, just nodding before bursting into tears. She kept mumbling about things, but the words were unintelligible from her crying jags.

Now the two of us were crying together.

"I have kidney damage, Soly," she said.

"Gaga, how... But Michelle's not contagious."

Bona sat on the sofa and switched on the electric fan because the house was starting to become uncomfortably hot from the noontime heat. "When I got fired, that's when the problems for me and Michelle started. Because I wasn't drawing any salary, Michelle missed one visit to the dialysis centre. The company benefits I received ran out after a few months, with some of them used for my credit card bills."

I could only stare at Bona while she detailed it all.

"Michelle wasn't with her father, Soly. She's also not

in America," Bona said, then paused for what felt like a long time. "Michelle's dead, Soly. She died after missing two visits to the centre."

It was hard for me to breathe while having to process Bona's admission. "How did it happen, Bona?"

"When I lost my job, I had nowhere to turn to for the dialysis payments. I was scared of what would happen if I missed one week of treatment. I couldn't do the Avon thing anymore because I failed to remit my collection. I had no way to contact Michelle's father; I don't know where he is. I pawned the TV, stove, jewellery, and lipstick, and sold all the unused Avon panties and bras I had in my wardrobe."

"But how did you get kidney disease?"

Ignoring my question, Bona continued, "When I already had nothing else to pawn or sell, I called up Myrna, the one from Accounting who gave five-six loans, to ask her where that clinic in Monumento was where people could sell one of their kidneys. That clinic that made rounds in jails, inviting inmates to sell their kidneys... Susmaryosep! I was desperate for money in those days."

I looked her in the eye, held on to her arm, and waited for her to refute what I had in mind.

"Yes, Soly, I sold one of my kidneys to pay for a few weeks of dialysis for Michelle. I just consoled myself with the thought that by doing so I could help another person needing a transplant. I only had one kidney taken out. According to the person who took it out, everything would still work out fine even if I only had one kidney, as long as I was careful. There are supposedly many people out there with just one kidney. I don't know what happened and how it came to this."

"Gaga, why did you do this?"

She smiled, wiped her tears away, and stroked her swollen midsection. She continued: "I was making Michelle's bed one morning. She smiled at me and said she felt so tired and just wanted to rest. So there! I let her be, switched on the television for her so she could watch MTV. By noon she was dead, with Madonna still playing on TV. Her face looked so tired, it had an 'I failed' expression. She died with her eyes open and staring at the ceiling."

On that day, which was also my birthday, I was supposed to share with Bona the news that I had been promoted. I decided not to tell her since it was in bad taste to mention the company she blamed for her child's death.

When the memo detailing the promotion was finally sent to me, I immediately returned it, enclosing my letter of refusal, to Ms. Dahlen.

"Why? Are you not satisfied with the compensation?"

I didn't say anything. I just looked at the mole on her cheek and her peculiar way of frowning.

"Ms. Castro, you are one of the assets in this company. You are highly skilled and can perform various tasks. You have a big potential for growth in this office." Ms. Dahlen moved her face next to mine, her arms extending across the table. "The company needs you to survive the competition. The industry is very competitive, especially now that foreign companies are around with their huge capital infusion. Please reconsider."

I could not get Bona's plight out of my mind. I remembered feeling sorry for her. And because human emotions tended to progress—or regress—in a certain way, pity was usually replaced by anger, sometimes even by hate as you sought out its source and roots.

There was a long awkward silence before I answered Ms. Dahlen. The memo for the promotion was still in front of her. We stared at each other for a long time. Nobody spoke. Nobody wanted to speak. *Deadlock, Dahlen*, I thought. I hated her so much I could not bring myself to say anything to her. I just walked out of the office, collected my things from my desk, and left the building without bothering to punch out of the Bundy Clock.

I quit my job at All Filipino Life Insurance Corporation that same day. I headed straight to SM Megamall to watch a movie which starred a Hollywood actor who was a favorite of mine and Bona's. Alone in the cold movie theatre, I told myself that life was short. Really short. ♦

Fungi

Biring's first contact with its slippery surface brought only momentary surprise: she stepped on it and slipped. It was sheer white, all too radiant under the plastic sachet of Tide Ultra. Her surprise turned to bewilderment when she picked it up. It was scintillating, even through the hair strands and clumps of pubic hair adhering to it. Biring quickly pocketed it, rushing to the dilapidated hut she called home. She secretly slipped it behind the altar. "There, right, nobody will see it there," she whispered to herself.

The next day, she invited her friend Buni to play with her at the itaas. She told her there was another truck carrying old fabric that they could scavenge to resell to the tailor at the corner outside of the Promised Land.

"Let's go, Biring," said Buni. "Let's play jump at the itaas."

According to the people of the Promised Land, she ended up being called Buni because when she came out of her mother, the first thing that the midwife assisting in her delivery noticed was the ringworm infestation that almost covered her left arm. She was said to be the only child in the Promised Land who developed ringworm rashes where the said fungal infection occurred in dense circular clusters.

Biring refused Buni's invitation, having lost her interest in playing. It was as if there was something that beckoned for her to return to the hut, to the altar, to the white thing behind it. "Buni, come," she told her friend. "There's something I need to show you."

"Why, how come you no longer want to play at the itaas? Let's go. We're better off spending our time there, where there's lots of discarded fabric for us to take."

"No, stay here," Biring exhorted. "I told you, there's

something I need to show you."

"What is it?"

"Magic," mumbled Biring.

Buni's eyes widened. "Really? Don't mess with me, or I'll beat you up."

Arriving at Biring's hut, the two decided to wait around until Biring's parents left to collect pagpag—leftovers from restaurants, including half-eaten meat cuts from the patrons—to be recooked for dinner.

Biring extricated the thing she hid behind the altar. "See here. It's magic, right?"

"Wow, Biring, where did you get this?" asked Buni.

"At the itaas, when I was scavenging for scrap metal."

Buni inspected it, carefully removing the hair strands and clumps of pubic hair on its surface. It shone even more brilliantly without all the hair stuck to it.

"It smells funny, Biring," Buni said. "Stupid, you should not have sniffed it!"

The thing, indeed, gave off a strangely pleasant smell. And the smell wouldn't come off their palms. Their hands were even tainted with whitish streaks.

"Hide this, Biring. Your father might take it. Can we sell it?"

"I don't know. I don't want to sell it. This is mine." She quickly secured it inside her pocket.

That night, Biring had a hard time sleeping. Her forehead was once again throbbing. And just like before, a rash was forming on that sore part of her body. It was always this way. There were days when rashes suddenly appeared on her body. The first time it happened was on her cheek, and her mother told her that it wasn't a rash but scales, like those of a fish. And it itched. It itched like hell. Her father said that her itchy scales were more than just scales. The next morning, while waiting for a truck from the countryside,

Buni noticed the pus suppurating from the scaly lesions on Biring's cheek. Buni wiped the pus away.

"Nanay said they were scales," Biring said.

"I had the same thing, too," Buni said, showing an infected part of her rump. "Oh, you also have scales."

"They tend to bleed when it's hot. Tatay said the yellow thing that's coming out of them is mucus," Buni explained.

"Will this go away?"

"Yes, I think so. All of us at home have it."

It did not surprise Biring to learn that her mother ultimately developed scales between her breasts, that her sibling had the same at the side of her mouth, that her father had his at the back of his ear. There were always nights when every single one of them was forced into wakefulness by the maddening itch of their scales.

Biring sat up and went to the altar. And because there had been no rain the preceding night, there was none of that sickly sweet stench inside the house. Her father likened the cloying smell to that of fermenting pineapple.

The Promised Land stank when it rained. The heady odour was produced by a combination of rotting food, rusting tin cans, vegetables, plastic, fabric scraps: all the broken castaways that were the sources of livelihood for Biring and Buni.

"What are you doing, you godforsaken child?" Biring's father called out to her when he saw her going to the altar. "Why are you still up?"

"Nothing. I just have to get something."

Biring could not help but bring the thing close to her nose so she could inhale that familiar odour again. The strong odour persisted long after she had moved it away from her nose. At one point, she noticed how the sweat from her palms made the thing more slippery to the touch and intensified its already overwhelming smell. She toyed with it some more, in awe of how its contact with her sweaty palms made it near-impossible to hold. It had grown slick to the point where it was like liquid slipping away from her grasp. The smell of magic was stronger now.

At first light the very next morning, Biring rushed to the itaas to tell Buni what she discovered about the thing.

"Really? Can we try it in water?" Buni suggested.

They headed to the lower part of the Promised Land, where the Spring was located. The Spring was in no way an actual spring, where pristine groundwater flowed. This supposed 'spring' was merely the stagnant, coffee-coloured water that collected around the base of a mountainous garbage dump. The Promised Land's touted Spring was the rainy season's runoff around the colossal pile of cloth fabric bundles, filth, rotting vegetables, empty tin cans, plastic bags, and plastic implements, castoffs that had outlived their usefulness.

"Go ahead," Biring told Buni. "Do it."

Buni plunked her hand in the Spring. Their eyes widened in surprise when they saw the dirty water around Buni's hand instantly turn white—not clear, but white. Buni swished the thing in her hand, just as Biring had done the night before.

Whatever it was that the two children started when they made the thing interact with water—it spread. It spread farther and farther, like the invisible magic of an invisible god, drowning out the suffocating stench of the Promised Land with its scent.

"Buni, there are bubbles! There are bubbles!" Biring jumped up and down with glee as the fetid water of the Spring began to bubble.

"Shh," Buni was quick to remind her friend. "Don't shout, stupid, someone might see us and take this away from us." Then she held out her hand, offering it to Biring. "Here, your turn."

Biring went through the same motions as Buni, and the

effects were the same. The two frolicked in their newfound fascination, slathering the water from the bubbling Spring across their cheeks, shoulder, forehead, thighs, and anywhere the water touched appeared to glow radiant. Its scent also clung to their bodies. In the days that followed, Biring and Buni continued to secretly bask in what they believed was the thing's magical powers.

"Buni, what's wrong with you?" Biring asked her friend when she once noticed her curled up with stomach pain.

"It really hurts. I can't take it anymore."

"When did that start? Did you eat the discarded food again from fast-food containers dumped at the Spring?"

"No. This all started when we used that thing."

"Stupid girl, did you put it in your mouth?" Biring began her victim-blaming.

"Of course not. Why should I, when it was bitter?"

"See, so you tasted it? How else would you know it was bitter?"

"But Biring, have you felt anything different since we started using the magic?"

"No, why do you say so?" Biring lied. Her skin felt oddly smooth and fresh the day they played with the bubbles made by the thing when it interacted with the dirty water of the Spring. Along with the refreshing feel of her smooth skin was the stomach-churning stench of the Promised Land. But it was as if her smooth skin resisted the greasy touch of the Promised Land's sickening air. What changed, though, was her heightened sensitivity to odours. And then her sense of taste. Latundan bananas, her family's usual dinner fare, made her nauseous. Her sibling also mentioned how she smelled differently. And each night, when Biring and her sibling had no choice but to fit themselves in their small sleeping area, she noticed how her sibling kept covering his nose.

One day, the two friends surprised all the people at the

37

itaas, who were scavenging and hawking their salvaged wares. Biring and Buni were covered up from head to toe, even their nose areas. Their fellow scavengers smirked. Some nodded with amusement and hurled profanities at the two.

"Don't mind them," Buni told her friend. "Them putang ina are just envious." That night, Biring excitedly accosted Buni.

"What's up? You have news?"

"See this," Biring said, showing her forehead. "My scales are gone!"

Buni stared in amazement. From that time on, they rubbed the thing any chance they got against their scaly skin.

At some point, they noticed something about the magical thing: it was shrinking.

"No, it's going to grow back to its normal size," Buni said with conviction, fervently believing what she said was true.

"I don't think so. Can't you see how it's becoming smaller and smaller."

The thing eventually shrunk to the size of an average thumb, which worried Biring.

"You said it would grow back to its normal size again. Why did you lie to me?" Biring sobbed as she confronted Buni, who did not know what to do or what to say as she was in a panic, too.

"What if we try to bury it in the soil, just like a seed growing into a tree," Buni said. "What do you say?"

And so, they planted the thing, dousing the ground where it was buried with water from the Spring. Days passed, and of course, nothing sprouted from the spot of ground they chose as the perfect place for growing the thing. And the longer they stayed at the Promised Land, the more unbearable the sour reek of the place became, the more nauseous they felt. The cloths covering their noses to ward off the nauseating smell became thicker and thicker. Their bodies ached for the thing's scent, how it had made their skin smooth, how it felt especially invigorating when they rubbed it against various parts of their body.

"Something's wrong, Buni. How come the magic thing hasn't grown yet?"

"Putang ina, I don't know. Should we dig it up?"

They did dig it up. Biring broke down, unable to find the thing in the spot of ground where they buried it.

"Where is it!"

"I don't know. Maybe it decided to leave us. Or maybe God took it. 'Tang ina, Biring. Our magic is gone."

"Do something, Buni, please do something . . ." Biring cried.

In the nights that followed, despair proved to be overwhelming for the two. They still could not get over the memory of the thing's slick surface, scent, and radiance. Each day that they pined for the thing, the more intense their hatred of their situation became—the festering, greasy feel of their skin, the nauseating fermented pineapple odour of the Promised Land, the flies that were attracted to them. There were even days that they closeted themselves in their respective huts. They could also no longer tolerate going to the itaas to scavenge for sellable items in the garbage dump.

"Buni, I have an idea," Biring told her friend one morning.

"What?"

"Let's hitch a ride in the garbage truck. We look for the magic outside. Someone might have taken it, or it could have found itself another Promised Land... I don't know. Bahala na! What happens will happen."

"You're so stupid. You know there's no way I'll be allowed to do that."

"Why not? It's your fault we lost the magic. You were the one who said we should plant it... because you have shit for brains!" Biring taunted her friend.

Buni remembered how it was, indeed, her suggestion to plant the thing in the ground. "Now what? Come with me."

"All right," Buni finally relented.

The two chose the last garbage truck taking the route to the Promised Land. Garbage trucks were scheduled to arrive at night in the Promised Land. Departure was at dawn. And because it was still dark then, nobody noticed Buni and Biring surreptitiously hiding themselves under the bundles of sacks and cartons.

"Pay attention to where we're going, Buni. We might not be able to find our way back," Biring whispered to her friend.

"Why are you always so stupid? Didn't your nanay and tatay tell you that all garbage trucks in this world end up in the Promised Land? If I ever get lost, it doesn't matter where I am in the world; all I need to do is hitch a ride in a garbage truck and surely I will find my way back to the Promised Land."

"How come I can still smell the pineapple smell of the Promised Land?"

"Because we're in a garbage truck!"

Alighting from the garbage truck, they were immediately struck by the familiar scent of the magical thing they thought they had lost and had to go out of their way to find outside the Promised Land. Their knees trembled with anticipation. They knew they were close to finding it. However, they had to settle for the subtle whiff of the thing's distinctive scent, which was often overpowered by the thick black exhaust fumes of motor vehicles. Interestingly, Biring and Buni could smell the thing on every person they encountered on the streets.

Slowly, they could no longer feel their gorge rising; they were no longer nauseous. The stink of the Promised Land was like a distant memory. The syrupy air? It dissipated with the dizzying view of skyscrapers. Biring thought the impossibly tall buildings looked like the thighs of derelict giants that lived in the clouds.

"Buni, look, a big Spring!"

"That's not the Spring... that's the Pasig River!" said Buni, with barely concealed pride. "I didn't know Pasig was this beautiful. What do you say we take a bath there later?"

"Tatay said it's deep. You know, he also told me that was where his mother and her three siblings went under when they were still kids," Buni recounted as she and Biring watched the grieving waters of the Pasig.

"Went under? Why?"

"Tatay said if your hunger pangs won't stop and when there's so much pain in every part of your body that it feels as if you and your body are two separate things, then that's when you should go under the Pasig River."

"But why? What did he say was in the Pasig?"

"The Mutya. Tatay said you should thoroughly wash yourself with clean water. The Mutya won't let dirty people in her domain. Tatay also said that the Mutya's dinner table is heaped with lots and lots of food. She's said to be rich and generous... as long as you've cleaned yourself well."

Biring contemplated Buni's recollections about the Mutya. "Do you want us to visit the Mutya?"

"How?"

"We just have to find the magic, and rub it all over our body. Remember its smell? I'm sure the Mutya will also like the smell," said Biring and then paused, realising the fact that they had yet to find the thing. "We have to find it first."

"I tell you, Biring, just like in my father's story, let me go under the Pasig if I can no longer take the pain of my empty stomach. Let me be the one to use the magic first."

"No problem. But what really happened to your father's mother and her siblings?"

"The Mutya did not allow them to return to the surface. They were given care and fed delicious foods. Tatay said that

41

whether or not he had stomach pains, he would still choose to go under the Pasig."

The two continued walking. They tried hard to track down the thing. They asked around, but people shooed them away. At night, they slept at the Pasig riverbank or lulled themselves to sleep by counting passing cars along Lawton Avenue. Whenever they were hungry, they ate food scraps in dump sites.

The city was unbelievably vast. The thing, on the other hand, remained diminutive and out of reach. This did not discourage the two, who barely remembered how far away they were from the Promised Land. As for the city, it kept changing what it wore daily: its outfits were always new and never boring.

Biring and Buni did not tire from observing the tall buildings, the vehicles that hurtled past them, the schoolbag-toting children on their way to school, the cars, the people inside the cars. All these seemed like an entirely different world to them. This was the world of enchantment. This was the one true source of the magical thing they were looking for.

One day, they passed by the foyer of a towering building. From the foyer came a gust of chilly air which seemed to beckon out to them. Entering the building's foyer gave one the sense that the entire world was reduced into a gigantic shoebox that could hold all the people in the world. The building's exterior was festooned with flags of various colours and designs. The chilly air welcomed them as they joined the throng of people entering the building. Biring nearly cried when she saw the high ceilings and sparkling fixtures, the mirrors that glinted with the truth—if only they could show her the truth—and the floor that appeared to her to be shifting in its shallow intake of breath. She saw her reflection in the mirrors, her hair taking on the colour of subsoil, her darkening eye bags, the in-and-out motion of stringy, dirt-encrusted tangles of nose hair. But it was the scent of the thing that the two found deeply enchanting.

"The magic is here," Biring said with certainty.

They followed the thing's scent trail. It took them almost the whole day searching. When they finally found the place where the scent was most pronounced, they stealthily snuck themselves in by timing the movement of the security guards stationed near the building's entrances.

"The smell's really strong here," Biring said.

"Yes, it's here. I can feel it."

They inspected every glass display stand. There were glass display stands for noodles, tinned goods, milk, and much else. They were amazed by the excessive displays, which to them represented the incarnation of another Promised Land. The wrapper design on every commodity was surprisingly familiar to them, too. Back in the Promised Land, instant noodle wrappers were strung into flaglets for Christmastime, the biscuit cans were either sold or used as dippers, buckets, or rice cookers, and the tin cans that could no longer be reused were flattened, weighed, and sold.

"Biring!" Buni called out when she found shelves filled with many different sizes and coloured variations of the thing.

It shocked the two to be faced with way too many pieces of the thing, the thing they called magic, gathered in one place. There's the thing in a box, in a plastic wrapper, in its bare form but decked with a red or pink ribbon. They wanted to stop the people from taking more and more of the thing to place in their grocery carts. Some were taking tens, dozens of the thing. One old woman was even pushing a grocery cart filled to the brim with boxes of the thing.

They could not even bring themselves to touch it. They were not the only ones who owned bits and pieces of that magic. Some people were even hoarding more of the magic than they deserved in this lifetime or the next. Biring could not help but cry at the unfairness of it all. She faced Buni, who was still stunned by the sight of person after person taking what used to be their magic.

"Buni, let's go. Let's get out of this place."

They sat, heartsick and sulking, among the beggars living near the Pasig. "What do we do now?" asked Buni.

"We have to be able to take home at least one piece of the thing."

"But how? We don't have—we don't have any money."

"We do what we do best. We scavenge the dump for items to sell."

"How do we sell them? Where? We can't just go back to the Promised Land."

"It's settled. We sell scavenged items."

"I have an idea," said Buni, making a dramatic gesture. She extended her open palm and made a forlorn expression. "I'm sure this will ensure we get one piece of the thing to take home with us."

Biring did not feel quite so sure of the idea. "I don't know. I haven't tried doing that before."

"Don't worry. We're simply going to try and see if we can get away with it. Besides, why wouldn't you want to get at least one piece of the magic?"

"I do want."

"All right, let's go by the roadside and beg for money."

Their plan of begging for alms commenced the next morning. They did it in front of Andrés Bonifacio's statue, the one that depicted the leader of the Philippine Revolutionary Movement with his hands on his hips, at the plaza right in front of the Philippine Post Office. The two extended their open palms, avoiding direct eye contact with the people passing by. With their necks and arms getting tired and numb from holding the same posture, they said over and over:

"One peso please, one peso please."

"Buni, are you okay," Biring said, worried about her friend who was lying curled up with persistent stomach pain.

"The pain's too much. I can't take this anymore."

"Squeeze down, squeeze it down tightly. That's what we do at home. We squeeze as hard as we can until the pain goes away."

"It hurts all over. I think the Mutya is calling me."

"Wow, Buni," Biring said, rising to her feet. "Lucky you. I think I must buy the magic as soon as possible."

She quickly slipped her hand inside her pocket. She searched Buni's pocket, too, and gathered all the coins they had managed to amass after hours of begging by the roadside. She crossed Lawton, walked the rear of the Metropolitan Theatre to reach the building—still pulsing with its chilly air—that held the thing they wanted the most.

But it was different this time. A security guard spotted Biring before she even stepped into the marble floor of the building.

"I'm only here to buy something," she pleaded to the guard.

"Get out of here," the guard said.

Biring showed him the pocketful of coins. She had faith in the money's ability to buy her the privilege of entry into the building. But the security guard harshly whisked Biring's proffered hand away, and the coins clattered across the floor. Biring bent down fast to retrieve the scattered coins, fearful of people snatching them. She didn't notice that nobody was paying attention to her or her money.

It was only when she was at a safe distance from the guard that she had the courage to hurl profanities. "Putang ina mo! Putang ina mo! I hope your eldest child dies!"

She walked, her shoulders slumping with the weight of her hopeless situation, back to the Pasig riverbank where she and Buni were encamped. Buni needed to be clean to face the Mutya... she had to be clean.

Walking the stretch of plaza in front of the Philippine Post Office, Biring bought a bottle of mineral water from a street vendor.

She came upon Buni wailing and clutching her stomach in pain. Buni's mouth was open in a garbled scream, shedding flakes of her cracked dry lips. Her eyes were rolled back, her legs shaking. Biring was used to this sight. Five of her siblings went through the same eyerolling and convulsions, the same agonised groaning finality of mouths impossibly stretched, so open that the flailing soul inside the body was already visible through the deep dark well of the throat.

Biring twisted the cap of the mineral water bottle, placing a few drops on her palm. And using her finger pads, she cleaned Buni, the dirty spaces between her fingers, her elbows, her knees, her toes. Using the hem of her clothes, Biring carefully rubbed the parts of Buni's body that were supposed to be clean so she could enter the Mutya's realm in the Pasig.

Buni's convulsion was still not letting up. Biring asked for Buni's forgiveness for her failure to buy the magic, which Buni so desperately wanted to rub against her body before presenting herself to the Mutya of the Pasig.

"They didn't let me inside the building, Buni. I was stopped at the doorway. Forgive me."

Because Buni could no longer stand up, Biring had to carry her. Biring was surprised at her friend's grossly lightweight body. It was like hauling a sack filled with plastic. Carrying her friend, Biring lingered in an area close to one side of the Pasig. She decided that by the next scheduled passing of an LRT train, she would release Buni to the Mutya. Biring, anticipating the train's arrival, pressed her chest hard against her friend's stomach in the hope that it would alleviate Buni's pain.

When Biring had the chance to glimpse her friend's face, she was struck by something she hadn't really noticed before: she and Buni resembled each other. Biring saw Buni's tears, and she could not help but weep as well.

"I will also visit the Mutya, Buni. Set aside some food at the feast for me." Biring took the LRT train advancing ahead as a signal to drop Buni in the Pasig River and turned away so she would not see the black water engulf her friend's body.

That night, she hitched a ride in another garbage truck, realising that Buni was right after all. Every single garbage truck in the world was headed to the Promised Land.

By dawn, she reached the Promised Land. She saw the crowd waiting for the truck's arrival, saw the same garbage mountain with its myriad colours, textures, sizes, aromas. Aromas that, when taken together, smelled sour, like rotting pineapples. Swarms of flies greeted her return to the Promised Land. She never forgot that this was the same exact place where she first found the thing of magic.

"Relief! Relief!" Shouts rang out. People ran in the direction of parked trucks. Biring also joined the rush of people.

An old woman handed to Biring a plastic bag full of relief goods. Biring immediately untied the knot and opened the plastic bag. She saw repacked bags of rice, canned goods, instant noodles, and a box of the thing that she and Buni were looking for. Once again, she now held the magic. She took a whiff, inhaled the pleasant smell. She started walking in the direction of the hut she and her family called home, lugging the plastic bag containing the relief goods and her magic. ♦

Beloved

This is what I keep saying to you: I'm sorry but I have to deal with this messy house, which is why I only saw you just now and can finally give you some attention. I can no longer take the sight of food morsels splattered along the edge of the sink, at the unfurled bundles of old newspapers under the dulang in the living room that I told you to throw away or sell a long time ago, in the foul-smelling bathroom every morning: how hard is it, really, to just use the stick broom to sweep the bathroom floor at night so that it's dry by morning? How come no one is interested in cleaning the house, and you alone are expected to be the one up to the task? You've been loitering all day.

I am sick of your complaints: "Always me, I am the *putang ina* you always see!" My reactions these past few days, please don't take them the wrong way. I only want to protect you, make sure you have a shot at a better future and have learned something from life, plus I don't want you to hang out with people in the backways and alleys, with Itoy and his pack of highway tricycle drivers.

It's not that I don't want to pay for your schooling. That's not the case. It's just that money is hard to come by these days; in this economy, it's so hard to find a job. That's why I'm asking you to not enrol, just for this semester. I don't have anything against you, and I most certainly don't want to back you into a corner. I hope you consider the fact that your Tatay's gone, your Kuya Ynel is jobless, the measly salary of an SM saleslady will prevent your Ate Almira from helping you with your school expenses. Nanay is old, so you can't blame her for the low sales at her corner in the wet market—and please don't expect her to do the cleaning around here. I don't get paid much, either, even if you see me every day wearing collared shirts when I go to work in Makati. You giving me the cold shoulder these past few days is hard on me, same with your refusal to take a bath with me and your avoidance of my kisses.

It's true what I said about seeing you inside the house only now, Junior. When we were kids, I spent most of my time studying and working hard, as the eldest, in order to be of use to this family. For example, I can help send you to school, which is what I'm doing as best as I can. You still remember Tatay? You were only a baby when he left to work in Iraq as a tinsmith and painter. Iraq, in those times, was at war with Saudi Arabia. Nanay was deathly afraid for Tatay's life, in that country that always seems to be at war ever since it came out of Mesopotamia. But Tatay had no choice but to stay in Iraq. He wanted to save enough money to be able to afford sending me to a private school when I reached high school. Things are different here, Junior. Here, in Luzon Avenue, parents draw their good reputation from the kind of school their kids attend. That's why I want you to finish college. See, Goring, Tatay used to taunt Nanay when he got drunk: "Even if you're just a market vendor, your Ramoncito goes to a private school!" But Nanay eventually managed to convince Tatay to return home from the Middle East. She told him that there were going to be four of us; the youngest was a boy. And that's you.

If there's one thing I hate about Iraq and Saudi Arabia, Junior, it's that they sent Tatay back home to the Philippines with a disease. Isn't it a fact that he got sick from that country? He arrived here sick with hepatitis because of the dirty water in Iraq. Although there was this one time when they were drinking, Engineer mentioned that Tatay might have gotten it from a prostitute, and Tatay simply grinned in response. He didn't quit his drinking habit until he developed cirrhosis. You were twelve years old when Tatay died. I know you also had a grudge against him in those twelve years: his drinking every night when he got home from work at the construction site, his beating up Nanay. Nonstop drinking even if body and eyes were already yellow.

Tatay wasn't a bad man, Junior. I hope you realise that. At least, he had some good in him. It was Tatay who taught us how to clean the house, to polish the floor using old candle wax, to shine the jalousies using wet newspaper, and many other tasks, from sweeping the toilet floor before going to sleep to unclogging the drain. Tatay never liked a disorderly and dirty house. Me, I just convince myself to see his drinking as his way of coping with his tiring construction job, and his physical abuse of Nanay, who manages the household budget, because of money issues. You've not experienced working nor having responsibility, so you don't have a concept of being 'pressured'.

Tatay did many good things, right? You remember our first time at Wildlife? In the lagoon, where you held on to my hand tightly. We talked about how we went with Tatay to EDSA to watch the showdown between Gringo's soldiers and the soldiers of the government. Nanay even had a fight with Tatay for taking us there, scared we would get hit by stray bullets from the coup d'état. But Tatay fought back, and tried to borrow money from a neighbour for our fare so the three of us could get there. We laughed like crazy in front of the lagoon. You already knew how to 'hold' hands. It also surprised me that you knew how to kiss. Until now, I am still hoping I can ask you who taught you to hold hands like that, to kiss that way using your tongue. I can barely recognise you because the house is such a mess.

I have lost track of your growth and your battle with demons outside the house, of your childhood to young adulthood. Back then, I was able to attend a private school. I was in school all day and consumed by schoolwork every single day. I also joined the school's theatre group, so I wasn't home even on Saturdays because I attended rehearsals. Sundays, I spent those in my room because Tatay and his buddies were having a drinking session in the living room. I hated Sundays back then. Then I got invited by a neighbour—by Jessa, who got knocked up by her own uncle in Purok Dos—to a Bible study group of American priests in a Purok Singko parochial church. They gave free snacks, plus a Bible and a rosary. And that was how American priests saved all my Sundays.

"Putang ina ni Tatay o!" was your Kuya Ynel's secret rant which he often let me overhear. "I'd have to clean up after them. The stink!" Tatay and his drinking buddies ate dogs, which reeked at room temperature, as well as cockfighting roosters sauteed in garlic. Your Kuya Ynel was also disgusted with the glasses and spoons used by Tatay's drinking buddies. How he resented Tatay, though he never made it obvious. How about you? Would you let Tatay know how much you hate him? Of course not. And nothing is achieved by that.

There's no future for sons and daughters who go against their parents, Nanay said. Always remember that.

I can't understand what's eating your Kuya Ynel. It looks like he's following Tatay's footsteps. When Tatay died, your Kuya sort of exploded from all the bitterness he allowed to grow in his heart. He was buying shabu from Aling Dulce's corner store, and right there would get high with his friends from the inner city, hanging out with the likes of Itoy. He didn't finish school, and was even jailed at a Balara precinct for selling marijuana! He became just like our male relatives and neighbours who can't handle their alcohol, run amok in the early morning hours when everyone's sleeping, and act all tough and angry as if they are up for a challenge. What's funny is that they only act tough on their own turf, not outside where someone can just as easily strike them with an arrow. They aren't willing to face up to someone brave enough to call their shit. They know they're safe on their turf because some of their neighbours are also their relatives. When your Kuya Ynel gets drunk, he has his own litany, too. "Teng-ena mot-Tay bakit mo kami enewan! Teng ina mot-Tay, lasenggo kang hayop ka!" A truly bold person, Junior, expresses what he really feels even if he gets spurned by the object of his emotional outburst. How do you measure courage but through fear, like love through hate? What is greater than love and courage?

Kuya Ynel and I used to share a bed. We used to talk all night, just like what you and I had been doing. One time he told me he wanted to be an astronaut. I laughed, and told him he probably didn't even know what 'astronaut' meant and had just picked up the term from Sesame Street. He got angry. "Tang ina mo, you think you're so bright because you're in a private school while me and Mira are only in Culiat," he said. For days at a time, he stopped sharing the bed with me.

Some nights after that, I saw your Kuya Ynel with Itoy. And that's probably the point where the gap between us was created: even though we didn't acknowledge nor discuss its existence, the gap continued to grow until we got used to it. Drifting apart became natural, like hair growth. We were too old to be sharing a bed. But still, there was a time we tried to assert our space inside the house, a space we could call ours, a space where we could hide to escape.

When we slept in the same bed again, your Kuya Ynel changed. Huh! It was the influence of the inner city. There were nights when my sleep was interrupted by movement from your Kuya Ynel aggressively playing with his cock. The bed was rocking, and it was hard for me to get some sleep. He did it almost every night. He knew I was awake because of my heavy breathing. I lost a lot of sleep, and it affected my schoolwork. There were mornings when our blanket had a fetid smell. The pillows and sleeping mat, too. One time, as I slipped inside the blanket, with him sleeping soundly on his side of the bed, I felt his icky sperm against my leg. It disgusted and annoyed me.

After that, I didn't sleep in the same bed with him again.

Nanay's role in the house remained the same, as a mediator of men who became unruly when drunk. Nanay assumed Tatay's death marked the end of this miserable situation brought on by intoxicated men. Your Kuya Ynel's drunken rages prompted Nanay's complaints in the barangay hall. With your Ate Almira, Nanay had to pay for Kuya Ynel's bail many times, too. Then the drugs hit Kuya Ynel, and it became worse: when he was high, he would go naked and run in the streets at night. Itoy and his friends could only laugh at his antics. Like a mad dog, your Kuya would go out without his clothes on. He would have crying jags, whining about his hate for Tatay for not sending him to a private school and all sorts of things. Your Kuya Ynel brought us so much embarrassment. You were still in grade school that time, so you were unaware of these things... or were you?

I was in college at the peak of your Kuya's dastardly behavior. I poured myself into my studies since I started getting the occasional snide remarks from Nanay about Ate Almira's desire to study Commerce. I became bitter towards Nanay for forcing me to adjust to the situation when all your no-good Kuya Ynel did was get busy on his drug habit. Nanay also downplayed my questions to her by saying that I was different compared to all of you: I take my studies seriously, I have focus and direction in life, I graduated from a private school, and I'm in a university. Back then, my responsibilities had already been spelled out in our chaotic household.

I had no idea where you were or what you were doing in those days; I didn't know what you had in mind, or whether life was kind to you. I saw you every day, I got to share a bed with you, shared the same rice plate from which we took our individual portions at the dinner table, but why was it that you barely made an impression then?

It is a shock to me to see you with an earring in your left ear, a nose ring, and a pierced tongue. You're getting older, and although we live in the same house, I barely notice: you're hanging out in the street corner with Itoy, you get home past midnight, Nanay is picking up rumors about how her youngest child has been smoking in front of Aling Dulce's store. I only discovered you've grown taller than me when we posed for a picture during my graduation from the university. We stood next to each other: me in my graduation suit and you wearing a polo. That picture was where I first noticed how much you've changed physically: your dimpled cheeks that call attention to your charming eyes just like Tatay, the veins in your hands becoming more prominent, your goatee and moustache. Like what I say to you whenever we go out and talk about that picture, about how it was like I was next to God, next to a very beautiful creature. You could only laugh and kiss me on the lips.

Your Ate Almira finished college. I went through hell and back—which I'm hoping you'll never have to experience—just to help realise your Ate Almira's dream. I did all sorts of jobs in many different companies to fund her tuition and school expenses. As for your Kuya Ynel, he ended up marrying your Ate Adela, who was already pregnant. He had no way to help with the expenses because he already had a family, although they have yet to move out and are still staying with us. It took three years before your Ate Almira got her job as an SM saleslady. She's not a regular employee but is always lucky to have her contract renewed every five months.

I told myself that since I'm 'done' with Almira, I could go to school again, to graduate school. My classmates from undergrad proceeded to either go to law school or graduate schools. You remember Dading? My one and only classmate who went to Tatay's funeral? He is well positioned at a multinational company in Makati. Dading worked from one company to another until he found the one that gave him his greatest break. I am not as adventurous as him and can't afford to be choosy with my employer. What if nobody hires me after? I can't have a break in my regular earnings, or Almira, who is still in school, will suffer.

"Nay, I also want to go to college," is how you appealed to Nanay in your attempt to shape your future. Nanay was forced to say yes, even though she knew we cannot afford it. Nanay met my eye, and I also had to say yes. "Sure," I told you, "As long as you study hard and do not squander our hard-earned money." I have a feeling Nanay was secretly pleased with me and my response. In fact, she's always pleased with me because I am responsible and practical, and she describes me as someone who will go places. That night, she approached me to say how thankful she was because I didn't turn out to be an outgoing type, because I didn't have a girlfriend, and was not thinking of getting married—that even through the cloud of her unspoken suspicions about me, she knew it would never get to that point. You're not a stranger to me, Junior. Again, I didn't do it because I feel responsible for the family's wellbeing—for you—but because I love you. Love has no room for invoking the debt of gratitude.

It was only at that moment that I started 'seeing' you at home, Junior. I hope you understand I have yet to get used to you being around, and that you and I still need to be reintroduced to each other.

But these past few months, you keep getting yourself mixed up with people from the bad side of town. Itoy is probably ecstatic about having company again, the fact that he's able to secure another victim from our family again. He is a no-good piece of shit. Now this is the first time I'll mention this to you. When we were young, Itoy did something terrible. (He lost his father at a young age, thus the lack of guidance.) What happened was: his father had gone out looking for a job in Morayta but never returned home. Itoy's mother claimed that he finally went with his mistress. But the neighbours, especially Tatay's friends, insisted that Itoy's father was picked up by the police after he joined the rioting farmers in Mendiola. He was killed in Parang, Marikina. Itoy also used to come over here to watch the noontime show *Eat.... Bulaga!* with us. He played teks with me and was my best buddy in every match: teks, goma, dyolens, and beetle fights during rainy days. I was in Grade One while he was in Grade Three, both studying at Culiat Elementary School. We walked to school together and did the same when returning home afterwards.

Itoy and I became good friends. We exchanged pamato for our bottle cap matches: I took the Pepsi bottle caps, while the Coke ones went to him. Itoy was great at flattening bottle caps using Tatay's hammer; the bottlecaps became lightweight like paper when shaken in the palm before pitching into the air. We always won with his bottle caps. We also always walked together all the way home from our class in Culiat. It was Itoy who punched my elementary school classmates who taunted me with "Gay! Gay! Ramoncitong badap!" I loved it when Itoy went after them one time while we were walking home from Culiat. They scampered like sewer rats being flushed out by the tanod. Itoy left us after driving away the other kids. I remember we were in front of a fire station in Tandang Sora and were walking home. "Just say you're not gay!" he told me, and I was crying and crying from Itoy's aggressive shaking as if to smack sense in me. He also threatened to let Tatay know that I was gay. And then he told Tatay.

It was a Sunday afternoon when Tatay, terribly drunk,

called me in front of his drinking buddies. He told me to stand on top of the dulang that became a catch-all for their empty Ginebra San Miguel and Tanduay bottles, discarded kalamansi rinds, and platter of kinilaw na dilis. His friends drinking with him that day had taken their shirts off, their chests red from the alcohol. "Pare, is your eldest really gay?" "Tang ina, pare, it's looking like you have two daughters!" Laughter. Tatay was livid. I was simply standing, facing all of them. I remembered how my ears felt warm from fear. Tatay summoned Itoy, the *damuho*, who was uneasy when he arrived at the house. "Why did you say my son is gay?" Tatay asked Itoy. "Is Monching really gay? Answer, or I'll circumcise you!" Itoy did not respond. "Maybe both of you are gay!" More laughter. Tatay told Itoy to take off his shorts. Intimidated by the drunks, Itoy did as he was told. "Hold his dick," Tatay told me. By that time, I was already in tears. "You don't want to do it? Maybe you're really gay. Go on, touch it if you're really a man!" I still didn't want to touch it. Tatay was scaring me with his hollering. "Naku, pare, your son might really be gay! What a lady!" They laughed, and laughed harder when Itoy's penis stiffened from all the touching from Tatay's drunk friends who said, "See, I am touching it and nothing is happening to me, I'm not getting hard... because I'm a man... But with Itoy, he's gay!" The men, especially Engineer, almost fell off their seats as they howled with laughter. "Aba! Manoy is getting angry! Is that how a real man should be?" Although Itoy kept his head down low, I could glimpse his buck teeth as he grinned. The men's 'merrymaking' was only interrupted when Nanay asked out loud if this was the sort of thing one would teach an eldest son. Nanay was holding you when she said *this* to the men.

After that incident, Itoy and I gave each other back our pamato. And since then, I have loathed all the Itoys of this world: loiterers, drunks, uneducated, dumb, living on the wrong side of town. This is why I can't see you become just like Itoy and it also proves how much I want you to finish college. I sincerely take no pleasure in having you stop school for this semester. Don't think badly of me. Pretty soon, I can get an SSS loan three months down the road, or I can get another job which pays a higher salary that's enough to pay for your schooling.

You keep saying that just because I'm older than you, my word holds water. That's not the case, Junior. I will certainly not limit possibilities for you as you need all the experiences this world has to offer. It's just that I'm hoping you will stop hanging out with those people, come home on time, clean the house when we're not around to do it, and generally be a good person. And don't bottle up your anger for any of us, or you might end up like your Kuya Ynel. Don't. And I'm hoping to see no more of your cold treatment of me.

Until next time, as I still have a lot of work to do. I'll see you later at Jollibee in Megamall. Wear the new Mossimo T-shirt I bought for you with my pay last month. But before you leave home, clean up the house; sweep the floor, especially the part under my bed where the dust has accumulated. ♦

Emilio Echeverri

"That man from Letran?" was what Betilda usually said whenever they reminisced about the good times at their former workplace where they all first met and became friends. Many in the gang would simply nod in agreement, while others would sport blank expressions as if they had desperately combed their memories for that man from Letran and come up with nothing.

"That man from Letran? The one who had a car?"

"How am I supposed to remember that man you keep mentioning, what with too many seamen sending their applications through the office?"

"The one from Letran. The one who drapes his polo shirt over his shoulder and leaves his white T-shirt untucked? You really don't remember him?"

The friends would exchange puzzled looks and try to recall the man Betilda was describing.

"You are such a pain in the ass, Betilda. Almost all the men entering the office were wearing white," said Marilou, who used to be the agency's receptionist.

Betilda was bothered by the fact that she was the only one who remembered Emilio. Sometimes, she could not help but think of Emilio as a ghost manifesting solely for her. But her speculation was instantly dashed by the memory of Emilio as a person who had a physical manifestation—that he had muscles and bones. Did Emilio have a soul? Emilio had a history that she'd read more than once from his nakedness, unluckily. She couldn't blame her coworkers for doubting his existence because she herself could only remember him as the 'man from Letran'. *The extent of my knowledge about him is probably this superficial*, she thought. When Betilda met him, he was a student at the Colegio de San Juan de Letran in

Manila, the educational institution which was closer to their office than the other schools and universities in Intramuros.

Because no one could remember Emilio, the topic of conversation would shift elsewhere. A waiter would be called to order the group's favorite—the one which, after drinking more than two glasses of weng-weng, packed a wallop equivalent to a horse kick—as well as San Mig Light for those who could not manage hard liquor. They would talk about their previous place of employment. They would clink each other's beer bottles and glasses, like former classmates having a reunion and going over prized memories from school. Laughing boisterously as if they were the only people in the bar. Their noise bothered no one, however, because the music was loud and bar patrons at other tables were rowdy as well. Through the noise inside the bar in Malate, none of them noticed they were already shouting at each other to be heard; they would realise it the next day with painful throats in the early morning.

After a shot or two of weng-weng, Betilda's favourite, she would slowly run her pointer across her forehead and think again about the man from Letran. Emilio. Emilio Echeverri. In her drunkenness, she would feel deeply disappointed with her former coworkers. *How come they can't remember Emilio? They used to talk nonstop about Emilio waiting at the lobby for me to get off work, and they made a big deal about the polo that he draped over his shoulder. They were also the reason I met Emilio. How come they can't all remember that now? Or is it because they refuse to remember?*

That time, Betilda had just transferred to Aces Maritime Agency in Intramuros. She had resigned from a consultancy firm in Makati because of the gruelling commute and the traffic along EDSA. The salary also wasn't worth it.

It was an overcast Friday. Betilda remembered that

during her interview with the HR manager, she was told that the agency was renting a building which stood on a lot right next to the old pre-World War II location of the University of Santo Tomas before it was transferred to España Boulevard. From the seventh floor of the building leased by Aces Maritime Agency, one could see almost half of Manila.

Intramuros is not as beautiful as Makati, Betilda thought while looking at the view outside the glass window of her new office. In Makati, the view consisted of skyscrapers and people, holding expensive briefcases and bags, scurrying like ants below. Ayala Avenue was always restless. From her time in Makati, where she worked on the office building's twentieth floor, Betilda developed a habit of gazing outside the office window every morning.

Whenever she felt like watching almost half of Manila's expanse, all she had to do was look outside the window. There she would see the cargo trucks coming and going from the pier, and taking up the entirety of the highway along Intramuros. There were also ferries crossing the Pasig River, ferries with rusting hulls. The river, even from afar, looked as if its pungent smell was potent enough to permeate the glass window. Its unsightly presence was offset by the nostalgic view of Escolta's old buildings. The sky had darkened then, which gave the illusion of the old buildings growing in prominence. They looked like rocks on the bank, rocks covered in moss nourished by rain or the whiff of decay from the dead river. Forlorn rocks mourning the death of their river.

"Are you going with us? Aren't you the new one at HR?"

Betilda smiled.

"Come on, join us. Ay! I'm Marilou, by the way. Receptionist."

"Betilda, HR assistant," she smiled and held out her hand to the receptionist.

Betilda was used to hopping from one company to

another, so she knew the main rule in every workplace: you need to learn to get along with your fellow employees, especially those who have been in the company for a long time. Without hesitation, Betilda said yes. She hurriedly went to her desk, tidied up the timecards she was auditing for the next payroll's payout, and slung her bag across her shoulder. In the lobby, their colleagues were already gathered for a night out. *This is fun*, Betilda thought. Among the people waiting for them were the accountant Tanya, the programmer Lynda, Irene from Betilda's HRD, and Eloy who was with Marilou at the reception counter.

"Girls, I want you to meet Betty from HRD," Marilou introduced her to the group.

One by one the women greeted her.

"So where to for our night out?" Betilda asked.

"Just here in Intramuros," said Irene, who was noticeably the oldest of the five. Almost all her hair had turned grey and she had lines on her forehead. Betilda knew about Irene's kid in high school and her OFW husband who left her for a domestic helper he had met in Dubai.

"Intramuros?"

"Haven't you heard of the latest night spots in Intramuros?" asked the surprised Eloy, the youngest in the group. She was wearing a flashy pair of earrings which had a sun and moon on them.

As soon as the group reached the lobby, rain lashed out and drowned the vehicular noise and road dust of cargo trucks headed for the Port Area. The angry drops drowned out the myriad noises and chaos of the city.

"Naku! It's pouring hard, friends. It looks like this won't stop anytime soon. How do we go about our night out now?"

"Don't worry, Betty, our destination is just a walking distance from here," Marilou said.

"The bar is just over at Puerta Isabel," Tanya shouted

amidst the din of the rain smashing against the parked cars in front of the building. The five companions unfurled their umbrellas and headed out into the rain. When they reached the bar, a waiter rushed to immediately welcome them. Since the women were regulars at Puerta Isabel, going there every Friday night, the waiters could instantly recognise them.

Even though it was still too early for the nightlife crowd, the bar was already too noisy, crowded, and smoke-filled from all the lit cigarettes. The noise was a combination of music, people having a great time, and clinks of beer bottles. The five women were seated at a corner table reserved just for them. Eloy started to slather foundation on her face. Tanya was scanning the crowd, looking for someone. Lynda, the programmer, was the quietest member of the pack; she sat next to the wall and was rummaging through her bag. Marilou raised her right hand to gesture for a waiter.

It was eight p.m. when a group of students arrived. Some of them were still dressed in their school uniform, while the others took off their polos and draped them over their shoulders. This was how Emilio was dressed when Betilda first saw him. The polo-over-the-shoulder thing became her go-to image of him in her memory.

The band started playing as soon as the group of young people arrived. The manager, an American expat and wife of the bar owner, likely saw them making their way into the bar. Everyone in the bar called her Mommy Yvonne, who also approached their table to introduce herself. When she saw the young men enter the bar, she instructed the band to start playing. People stood up, went to the middle of the stage at the centre of the bar, and started dancing. Betilda just noticed Marilou, Irene, and Tanya at the dance stage. Eloy looked like a mad dog that had escaped, shaking her head every which way to the music. Lynda stayed in her seat, looking as if she was searching for someone in the crowd.

Betilda was convinced that as soon as she finished her first shot of weng-weng, they would see that she was the queen of raves in Malate, Makati, or Libis. And she could not deny this as she was well-known in the various Manila parties.

When Betilda felt the effects of the alcohol in her soul and she began to go lightheaded, she took off her blouse, revealing a blue sleeveless top. She rushed to join the people on the dancefloor, and her friends erupted with wild cheers to welcome her. Her thoughts drifted, and she felt the weight in her chest lifting. It was dark inside the bar because Puerta Isabel's pillars had turned grey with age. The concrete had blackened, resembling the gums of a raging old man knocked down by age as an impotent, an old man powerless against young people's rowdiness and ceaseless dancing to trample the sacred and tender memory of his youth. Moments later, the band stopped playing and music from the DJ's booth blared across the room. The DJ began his blather, and it was greeted with earsplitting cheers from the crowd. Puerta Isabel shook with the noise. Dance. Dance. Gyrate. Hips. Head. Part the thighs. Expose the bellybuttons. Go on. Bite your lips while swinging. Release. Release. And the cheers expunged every last bit of modesty outside the mind, outside the body along with the beads of sweat on the skin. Nobody noticed the rain had stopped. The lights went out, and out came the colourful glowsticks.

There was red, blue, and purple. Some of the glowsticks were worn as necklaces and bracelets, while the others were clutched inside mouths. The young men who had just arrived joined the people on the dancefloor. It was at this point individual histories seemed to no longer matter—everyone's differences, even their social class, their personal beliefs and mindsets, were suddenly rendered moot. The only thing important in this sensory feast was the present reality.

Forgetting could heal the deepest cut in the soul of the restless youth. Strangers danced with each other. If you were a woman, you would respond to a man touching your navel with a caress on his nape.

People returned to their seats when the music stopped. The friends were happy. Betilda was dead tired from dancing.

"You dance really well." A man approached the five women, all slumped from exhaustion in their seats.

The women looked at each other. Eloy grinned. Marilou signalled to Tanya by tapping Tanya's thigh. Lynda pretended to search for something in her bag. Irene held out her palm to say she's too old for flirting with young men.

"I'm Emilio," said the man holding a beer. "I noticed that you dance well. Did you go to The Rave in Malate last week?"

"Yeah," Betilda said in a petulant tone.

The women giggled. Betilda wished to see Emilio's face clearly, but she was too drunk to focus and there was darkness shielding his face.

Marilou elbowed her, goading her to respond to the flirtation.

This was one of the things that unsettled Betilda. Regardless of how many times she described what happened that Friday three years ago at Puerta Isabel, the group still had no recollection of Emilio. How come they couldn't remember? Or maybe they were feigning forgetfulness.

"Oh, Betty, looks like you have a lot on your mind. Are you drunk? You only had one shot of weng-weng," said Marilou, baffled by Betilda's quick slide into drunkenness.

"Don't tell me you're thinking about that Letran dude again?" said Lynda, who was getting married next month, in a teasing way.

"You really cannot remember?"

Everyone in the group sighed simultaneously in response.

"You're too far gone, Betty. You might end up like Eloy. Don't use too much, go easy on it... the 'factory in Sagada' won't be closing anytime soon," Tanda said, referring to Eloy's stint at a rehabilitation centre one year ago for her addiction to drugs and marijuana.

"Gaga! I'm not that crazy. Eh, if that's the reason people become forgetful, then maybe that's why you can't remember that man from Letran."

"Why were you thinking about that man, anyway? What happened to you?"

"Marilou... you, of all people. It's like you didn't know," Betilda said with a smile.

"But there's nothing you told me... us..."

It was not exactly true about Betilda withholding the story from them. It was noon in the office pantry when she told them about her one-night stand with Emilio after that rave. They all even giggled suggestively as Betilda gave them the lowdown about what happened between her and Emilio inside his car at Remedios Circle in Malate.

They smoked a joint from Sagada before having sex. Emilio was in the driver's seat, with Betilda riding him. She never forgot that night and how Emilio's hot breath explored her body. From the neck, the hips, between her breasts. Emilio switched on the radio, playing loud music while they did what they knew about merging their histories.

Marilou, Irene, Eloy, Lynda, and Tanya did enjoy hearing all the steamy details from Betilda. So their collective denial of Emilio's existence struck Betilda as odd.

There were days when Emilio could be seen at their office lobby, where he waited for Betilda to get off work. But mostly he preferred to wait for Betilda at the reception area of Aces Maritime Agency on the seventh floor. He would wait for her and drive her home, or sometimes the couple would attend another rave in Malate or have dinner in one of the restaurants in Muralla. Emilio was always seen waiting for her, especially during Fridays when he wanted to drink away his worries. Many people did see Emilio. Irene would sometimes go over to Betilda's office table just to say that 'her man' was here and waiting, with Betilda simply laughing it off in response.

One time, Emilio got so impatient with the long wait that he turned to the seamen in a queue for their applications to be processed. But there was something about Emilio that set him apart from the other men at the reception area. Betilda noticed this as she observed him from afar. From the way he gestured when he spoke to his habit of draping his polo over his shoulder, he had a self-assured air about him. Betilda felt a stirring in her loins as she watched him.

Emilio's hair always looked wet from his hair gel. Even at night, he always looked as if he had just stepped out of the shower. One other thing about Emilio that didn't escape Betilda's notice was the fact that he did not seem to perspire, like he always looked fresh and clean. For Betilda, Emilio was the man with narrow eyes, a mestizo with dimples. She could not get over taking in his face and his quizzical, judgy expression.

She asked him a lot of times about himself, but he kept changing the topic whenever it touched on his family or history. Or he would kiss her to shut her up.

One night in a bar in Puerta Isabel, not the same bar managed by Mommy Yvonne, Betilda asked him drunkenly: "Emilio, if you had one wish, what would it be?"

"Simple. I would wish for a perfect love, a perfect truth, and a perfect happiness."

They laughed. A casual observer would mistake them for lovers.

Work at Betilda's office was once suspended because the Philippine president attended a banquet at the Manila

Cathedral. Employees were sent home early so that some of them could attend the event as well. That was a Monday, and it was only two in the afternoon, too early to hit the bars in Puerta Isabel. Betilda decided to go home and rest as her previous night was spent at a classmate's birthday party.

For some reason she took the Baluarte de San Gabriel route, a path north of Intramuros. The Baluarte route was the fastest way to Lawton, which meant passing in front of Letran. Betilda was on her way to Lawton to get a cab. Letran's main entrance was packed with students, and haphazardly parked all around were the cars of teachers and students. She saw Emilio in front of a restaurant. He was wearing sunglasses, his trademark polo draped over his shoulder. She was dubious at first about whether it was really him, but she recognised the unique way he moved, his posture, his wrist that was like the branch of a spritely tree. His breast. No doubt it was him.

Betilda was about to approach Emilio when a man came up to him and whispered something in his ear. Emilio quickly said goodbye to his friends, the same group of students who'd been with him the first time Betilda saw him in Mommy Yvonne's bar. Emilio and the man huddled by the side of the restaurant. The man was noticeably much older than Emilio, wearing a collared polo and denim pants. The man talked with his mouth close to Emilio's ear, patted the young man's shoulder and handed him some cash. As Betilda excitedly walked closer to them, she could finally see the older man as he leaned to whisper something again to Emilio. She figured the older man was Emilio's father, though she found him to be unabashedly effeminate. She could not shake off the impression that Emilio's father might be gay. The next thing the older man did surprised her. She saw him touch Emilio's smiling face. And it wasn't just a touch, more like a caress. The older man eventually left, his car hurtling outside Baluarte de San Gabriel. Emilio saw her and waved. She could only stare back at him, wanting so badly to just walk the other way, but found it hard to leave. She regretted showing herself. She waved back and said, without thinking: "Hi! Oh, where to tonight?"

They got drunk again that night at Puerta Isabel.

"Emilio, I'm just curious. Can I ask you something?" Betilda pried as they drank weng-weng, which became Emilio's favourite through all of Betilda's exhortations.

"So what if I'm still a virgin," Emilio joked, and both of them laughed.

"It's not that. I already know the answer to that, gago! I must ask since you have a peculiar name. Are you Spanish?"

"Ah, that Echeverri? There's Spanish on my father's side. My father's family is based in Negros."

"Don't tell me you came from a landlord clan? You as rich as Erap?"

"Yeah. But Betina—"

"Gago! Betina what? You can't master my name until now?" she said in a good-natured ragging.

"Oh, shit!" He rubbed his hands against the sides of his head. "I'm sorry, I'm not good at memorising names."

That ended their conversation. It was past midnight when they exited the bar and went to Emilio's car. They did their usual: smoked a Sagada joint and had sex in the cold, cramped, noisy interior of Emilio's car.

"Yes, I remember that! I remember you talking about your escapades inside some guy's car. I'm just not sure if you meant that guy from Letran." Marilou was almost shouting, as she was already way too drunk. "And besides, how am I supposed to remember that when I couldn't even count how many times I did it with my boyfriend!"

That drew laughter from the rest of the group. Betilda scratched her head in frustration and was close to giving up on her friends' continued denial.

"What if that man is a ghost of Intramuros?" Tanya taunted.

"What ghost?" Betilda said, annoyed.

"A ghost," Marilou said. "Pulgas, the building's security guard, had stories about the ghosts of Intramuros coming out to haunt because they were disturbed by the noise of the new bars around Muralla, the weekly raves. And they were angered by the renovation of the rows of buildings in Puerta Isabel to make way for bars and restaurants. Isn't that where you met that man from Letran?"

"He can't possibly be a ghost," Betilda said, visibly flustered and irritated. "He had a body, you've met him. We saw each other many times and he even went to the office. How can he be a ghost?"

"Because you are the only one who has a memory of him! Punyeta!" Marilou said angrily.

"Drop the topic! Drop the topic, please..." Irene pleaded.

"All right, no more discussions about that man from Letran," Tanya said. "And please, let's avoid topics that remind us of the agency that retrenched us. Erap only got ousted. It wasn't fair that we lost our jobs!"

"Yeah. Bad memory. Drop the topic," Irene said. "We have a new president. There is hope." Then she laughed at her own joke.

Emilio Echeverri could not possibly be a ghost because he had a body. He had flesh and bones. History could be read from his nakedness. Emilio could not be a ghost. Is there a ghost that could wait in front of McDonald's? Liked Nike and shades? Barhopping? MTV? But how come they couldn't remember Emilio? Why?

Betilda herself only had a vague memory of how she and Emilio parted ways. All she could remember was that she got fired and then went to work for another agency in Makati. They never saw each other again after that. She also didn't visit Puerta Isabel again because Intramuros was too far from her new office. Betilda could remember the last night they went out drinking and then ended up in his car to rest for a while before going home. It was almost dawn, and they were parked in the part of Puerta Isabel that had a good view of Letran's hallway as well as the restaurant next to the school. She jokingly asked Emilio again about what his wish would be to Ronald McDonald as a magic clown. They used to eat at McDonald's because it was open in the early morning hours. "A perfect love. A perfect truth. A perfect happiness," Emilio said and sighed.

Her expression blank, Betilda stared at the TV suspended on the bar's ceiling. She scrutinised the shifting layers of colours as the scenes changed on MTV. She stared at the colours, unable to hear the music because it was drowned out by the song from the DJ's booth and the people's revelry. A part of her wanted to jump and move with the beat on TV. *Yes, I want to dance. I will dance. I will dance!*

"Hey, Betilda! What's on your mind again? Is it the guy from Letran?" Marilou slurred drunkenly.

"Ah, no. No."

"What's with the seriousness?" Irene said.

"Stop thinking so much," Tanya said.

"Ah, no. No." The shot of weng-weng coursed through her. "No. I was thinking how there's going to be another retrenchment. I have no idea where to work next."

"Ah, is that so?" said Lynda, finding at last the lipstick she kept rummaging around in her bag for, and painted her lips red. ♦

All the Quiet Sundays

All the Sundays at home had grown quiet after Porboy was buried some twelve years ago. My mother, a young widow, did not remarry. Everyone was there at Porboy's funeral, accompanying my father to his final destination: the grave. My father was laid to rest on a Sunday, like fate's final joke on him. I could not forget that day; everyone was in black, grieving and trying to console my mother. Over there were the pictures taken during the funeral, carefully arranged in a photo album unopened for almost a decade and buried under stacks of books stashed inside Porboy and Nanay's former wardrobe closet.

"I got a letter yesterday. Your Ninong Andy is returning to the Philippines next Sunday. He will visit us before going home to Negros," Nanay told me one morning when I arrived home from the office; I worked nightshifts at a call centre. Nanay was opening her store, putting the soy sauce on display, the sugar in plastic retail packs, the charcoal and mung beans in cellophane bundles. Ever since Tatay died, Nanay had taken up her street corner vending seriously.

"Ninong Andy? The one in Saudi?"

"Yes, he's set to come home." Nanay's expression soured, because she knew the burden of attending to a guest, much like the burden we had shared for a long time when Porboy was still alive. "He says he wants to see you."

"Why me?"

I know Ninong Andy—but only in name. I could not even visualise his face in my mind because there was no picture of him at home. Porboy talked about him many times. I also heard Porboy mentioning him to his drinking buddies. When I was christened, Ninong Andy supposedly stood as my godfather. He was also Tatay's fraternity brother at

UNO-R. Porboy ran away from his home in Bacolod, braved Manila in 1978, and never came back to Negros. I was born in 1979, and according to Tatay, it was 1983 when Ninong Andy went to Saudi Arabia. My father said that the last time he saw him was before he ran away from Bacolod. "How can I possibly be the godson of a person who wasn't even in Manila when I was christened?" I once asked Porboy, and I couldn't remember whether or not he answered my question.

"Why can't Boyet pick him up from the airport?"

"No need to pick him up. He said he will be staying in Taguig. He supposedly had friends living near here, likely in Culiat, in Tandang Sora. He said he will come over by Sunday afternoon. You need to be here—your ninong wants to see you."

Ninong Andy would be here on Sunday, the favorite day of Porboy as well as his buddies and coworkers at the construction site. "Boyet will be home. I won't be here next weekend. I have a teambuilding with my agents in Batangas." The truth is, I dreaded the prospect of meeting and having to spend time with the visitor. I had no idea what we would be talking about, what alcoholic beverage to offer him, what his preferred food to go with alcoholic drinks was, and the one thing that troubled me most was my dislike of alcohol. If I should drink with him, I wondered how that would go as I had no idea who he was. It was Boyet, my youngest sibling, who was the only one fit to be in the company of Porboy's guest.

"As for you, Brando, your ninong just wanted to drink with you. Why don't you buy that—what was that they used to drink, that expensive alcohol?"

"Black Label."

"Yes! But he might bring his own Black Label just like your father—Black Label from Saudi." Nanay could still remember all of Porboy's liquor purchases from Duty Free at the airport; my father used to brag about secretly buying alcoholic beverages sold at high prices from a Jeddah black market and drinking them while in Saudi, where Muslim culture forbade alcohol consumption.

There were five more days before Ninong Andy's arrival, which was enough time for me and Nanay to prepare for Sunday's drinking session. Nanay and I were sure that Porboy's visitors would arrive in droves on Sunday, just like when he was still alive. Back then, they came in hordes every Sunday, all of them Porboy's fellow construction workers. They worked for six days straight as tinsmiths, painters, carpenters, masons, and sometimes stay-ins for a building under construction, so they treated Sundays as sacred. This was why Nanay and I were so sure Ninong Andy would not come alone. And this Sunday, Nanay and I both saw the need to be ready with several bottles of San Miguel, food to go with the drinks, and wide enough space in the living room for the empty beer bottles and passed-out bodies of Ninong Andy and his friends—who were most likely also Porboy's friends— after drinking all afternoon and throughout the night.

Nanay and I knew exactly what would happen this Sunday. We also knew the preparations for that day—all of which we learned from Porboy and his fellow construction workers who used to arrive home with him for their Sunday drinks—everything from clearing the platters heaped with peanuts, the ripped plastic containers of chicharon, and the beer bottles, the mopping up of vomit, spit, beer spills and ice bucket splashes, to the careful rearrangement of the passed-out bodies of intoxicated men. All this took up the wee hours of Monday mornings or Sunday afternoons. So, for Ninong Andy's arrival, even if it was more than a decade since Porboy's last Sunday on earth, we could still perform these same old rituals.

I could not pinpoint exactly when during my childhood this particular Sunday routine of Porboy's began to take over our home. What I remembered was that Porboy started to have me run errands while I was in first grade. He would ask me to buy bottles of San Miguel Grande, some bottles of gin, a few pieces of kalamansi, some food, and sticks of Hope Menthol. What I remembered was that by the time I understood what 'drunk' meant, these Sundays were already part of my life as well as my mother's life with Porboy.

But according to Nanay, and also to my father's sisters who used to live with us when they were still single, their Sundays with Porboy began long before I was born, before my parents got married. Porboy drank with his friends at Central Market when he was still in Negros, in Bacolod. They said my father learned to smoke and drink alcohol at a young age. Many times, he had to be dragged to his house in Mansilingan because he was too drunk to walk.

It was Tita Belly who told me all about Porboy's misadventures in Negros when he was growing up. I was already in high school when Tita Belly arrived at our house in Luzon Avenue. Tatay's youngest sibling came to live with us to help Nanay take care of me and my brother. Nanay was busy selling fish at the market while Tatay worked outside the country. Nanay already had her space at the market then, while Porboy worked in the construction of a hospital in Jeddah. It wasn't from my father that I first heard of Ninong Andy. It was Tita Belly who introduced my ninong's story at home.

It was hard for me to forget Tita Belly, the youngest of eight siblings on my father's side; Tatay was the fifth child, a middle child. "Porboy is a black sheep," Tita Belly would repeatedly scoff about Tatay. "So you really have to study hard. Your father failed to graduate from college because of his friends and vices. That's why he's called Porboy."

Tita Belly was fat, preferring a bob when styling her hair. She was always smiling pleasantly, too, and had the habit of cleaning the house right after waking up in the morning and then in the afternoon before dinner. She also did the laundry and picked up Boyet from school. And unlike Porboy who skipped school at UNO-R and went to Manila, Tita Belly finished college. One of her chores included helping me with my homework and disciplining Boyet and I whenever laziness hit us.

"You, Brando, take your studies seriously," Tita Belly used to nag me back then. "Your father is slaving over in Saudi just to get you through a private school." This was what she kept telling us; the fact that we were in a private school supposedly translated into a topnotch education. "Unlike him who was an undergrad... look at Brando's Ninong Andy who completed his course at UNO-R." This was how Tita Belly introduced Ninong Andy to me, by contrasting him with Porboy's life's failure "because of friends and vices."

"Your Ninong Andy was in Saudi Arabia way before your father got there and he also already saved enough for their house in Mandalagan. But I had no idea if your father met with him there... Because that Porboy is such an ass, who even had the nerve to snub your Ninong Andy after what Porboy did to him."

Tita Belly did not completely open up to me about the details of what happened between my father and Ninong Andy. Whenever I asked Tita Belly about that, she would respond with nothing but a physical description of Ninong Andy, who was said to have been tall with narrow eyes, a broad chest, and a high-bridged nose. "I don't know if he gained weight or developed darker skin, but your Ninong Andy was not known to neglect his body when he was in Bacolod. Blackbelt in karate... like your father. I'm not sure, though, if your father got together with him in Jeddah." And whenever I asked whether there was conflict between Porboy and Ninong Andy, her immediate reply would be: "Because that Porboy is such an ass, who even had the nerve to snub your Ninong Andy after what Porboy did to him."

Tita Belly lived with us for a long time and became Nanay's collaborator in running the household. And because Nanay did not have basic formal schooling and Tita Belly was a college graduate, they were perpetually at odds with each other. It was Tita Belly, for instance, who snitched to Tatay about how Nanay had been squandering the money he sent from abroad on household items like a table, a TV, and expensive kitchen implements. And since Tita Belly was Tatay's youngest sibling, his tendency was to believe what she said.

On the day Tita Belly was set to move out of the house, I remembered her having an argument with Nanay. Not the kind where there was screaming. They talked directly facing each other and exchanged words loaded with mutual rage. What set them off was Nanay taking on a debt from the Bombay moneylender for a massive glass-framed reproduction of *The Last Supper*. Nanay planned to decorate the living room with it.

"Why do you need that, Elena? Does Porboy know about this?"

"I'm the one who wants this. And one more thing, this is a five-six from Bombay."

"Maybe you're forgetting that your husband is not in Saudi for a holiday vacation."

"Maybe *you* are forgetting that I am the wife and this is my house."

This was how their argument ended. Tita Belly left right after lunchtime. She did not say goodbye to us. This was also how her almost three-year stay with us ended. She returned to Negros and has lived there since. Tita Belly had never gotten married so stayed with her eldest sister. When I finished college and was able to get a job in the marketing department of an IT company, I was assigned to Bacolod

City. So after nine years, I saw Tita Belly again. I met her at Apollo, even offering to pay for what we ate. She still wore the same old bob but it was all too apparent how every single bit of her youth had vanished, as well as the fact that she was ill. She was 30 years old then and had ovarian cancer.

"Because your mother is Waray," Tita Belly said when I asked her if she could still remember that fight with Nanay. "Who buys *The Last Supper* for the living room? I'm glad you finished school, otherwise you'd be just like your mother and her relatives in Samar." Five months after our get-together, Tita Belly passed away. I was already back in Manila and not able to pay her my last respects.

Everything went down south when Porboy came home. Of course, he was angry over what had happened, over Tita Belly being forced to leave home and go back to Negros. He trained his rage at what he felt was the source of all this: the framed print of *The Last Supper* from the Bombay moneylender. One Sunday, a completely drunk Porboy grabbed it from the wall and smashed it against the floor. Broken glass was strewn all around and the picture was slashed down the middle. It was Sunday night, and the boxes of chocolate bars, biscuits, and clothes that he had bought for us were still unopened. After smashing *The Last Supper*, he went after the plates in the kitchen, punched a hole in a cabinet that Nanay bought on an installment basis, and kicked the TV. "You really think I was just having a great time abroad and didn't work my ass off? You think you are a rich donya? You think my life in Saudi was easy?" And when there was nothing else for Porboy to smash, throw, or kick, he aimed his rage at Nanay. He was really drunk, and I couldn't take my eyes off his chest. There appeared to be a red triangle sticking to his skin, with one of the triangle's tips pointing directly at his navel. He grabbed Nanay's hair and was about to slam her against the living room wall, that bare wall that had been left with no finishing layer because he wasn't able to send enough money before his trip back to the Philippines, when Nanay slipped away from his grasp and ran to the neighbour's house. A neighbour, who was Nanay's distant relative, carried Boyet outside the house, leaving me perhaps because they thought since I was already in high school, I was old enough to run and save myself from the enraged Porboy. After Nanay left, I rushed to my room, locked the door, and sat on the table that Tita Belly bought for me so that I had a place to do my schoolwork. I opened the first book I could grab from the neat pile of books on the table. And I read and read.

Then I heard his friends, the same ones from the earlier drinking session, return to the house to pacify him. I heard how one of his friends asked to buy another bottle of gin. Their routine to calm Porboy down during his drunken rages was to give him more liquor to knock him out. It took them almost an hour. I went out of my room when I knew Porboy was already asleep on the sofa and all of his friends had left. And just like any Sunday night or early Monday morning, I cleared up and collected the glass used for the tagay where everyone drank from the same glass, the San Miguel bottles, the plates and saucers of greasy, putrid stews of dog, pork, or rooster. I went out of the room to do the Sunday ritual. I saw Nanay in the living room. She was kneeling before Tatay's luggage, the boxes of gifts for us. Silently, slowly, and very carefully as if they were breakable crystals, she unpacked the contents of the balikbayan box.

"Have you already bought the San Miguel?" Nanay asked. What she actually meant was whether I had already bought a case of grande, that bottle of alcohol that was almost one litre in size, the one intended for group drinking.

"Two cases. I guess this is more than enough in the event Ninong Andy comes with his friends," I said. I also bought a shank, two roast chickens, and ice. He was supposed to arrive at one. Boyet, because it was Sunday, decided not to leave the house to have drinks with Ninong Andy and I.

"It's been a while since I saw Andy. He's good looking, your ninong, fair-skinned. Tall and a karate blackbelt," Nanay said. I could feel her excitement. "Andy sent us some money when your father was hospitalised. But I didn't tell Porboy. You know his pride."

"Did we buy too much beer?"

"No! He was in Saudi for many years. A decade of no alcohol and pork... you know how Muslims are."

Nanay said that it was possible Ninong Andy had become too rich because of how long he had worked in Saudi. She also said that he had been married when he was young, just like Porboy, and had three kids, and the eldest was my age. On top of sending money for Tatay's hospitalisation, he also sent some when Porboy died. All this Nanay recounted to me while I was making preparations for Ninong Andy's arrival. I had no idea my father and Ninong Andy used to be tight as friends. The rift between the two was what I did not understand, and found most intriguing. What did Ninong Andy do to Tatay? And why was it that the more Tatay drove Ninong Andy away, the more intense Ninong Andy's efforts became to mend fences with Tatay. Nanay was tight-lipped and gave only a curt reply when I asked her about it. "Your father's pride got in the way. He and his pride were inseparable even in death." End of story.

But it was true, what was said about Porboy's pride. Every time he got drunk, I would hear him ramble on about his life's disappointments—like his failure to finish his UNO-R schooling. According to Tita Belly, he took up a course in Civil Engineering but was constantly prevented from finishing it by his vices, friends, fraternity, and quarrelsome ways. His parents, my grandparents who were in Cadiz back then, only knew about him no longer going to school through a letter he sent them to say he was getting married in Manila.

"If only I finished college," Porboy often said. "My life wouldn't be like this."

I saw the sorrow in his eyes when he fell ill. His ruefulness was more likely due to the fact that he could no longer consume alcoholic drinks. He had quite a reputation as a bad drunk, and for some reason he thought he could no longer face his drinking buddies in his current condition: the great wild drunkard with his intoxicated rages, now a shadow of his former glory because of his diseased liver. Since then, all of the doors and windows at home remained closed because Porboy didn't want the neighbours to get a glimpse of him bedridden on the living room sofa. He also avoided going outside the house or meeting his friends. He would only consent to be taken outside or leave the hospital at midnight, so people would not see his yellowing skin, his swollen body, his bulging eyes.

The image of Porboy during his final night was what stayed with me. I had just got home from the university. Entering the living room, I noticed him on the sofa and he was sitting up, his head almost dangling from weakness. He held a glass of gin. I slammed the door shut and walked towards him. I knew he was looking at me because I could feel the weight of his gaze. Lugging my bag and books, I approached his place on the sofa slowly and without glancing at him. I stayed in my room and did my schoolwork. I kept the door closed and was uneasy throughout, knowing that Porboy was in the living room drinking gin. Close to midnight, I went to the living room to watch TV. He was still on the sofa but was already lying down on his back. Nanay had cleared the glass and bottle of gin. I was seated in front of the TV. I knew he was still awake behind me.

"You should turn that off," he said. "It's late, and people are sleeping. You always think only of yourself."

I switched off the TV and returned to my room. By morning, we all woke to Nanay's screams. Tatay had already passed away. Porboy was dead. The neighbours came by, gave their condolences, cried with Nanay. I got up from bed, shuffled towards the bathroom, took a bath, got dressed, and attended my classes at the university.

Boyet was rushing as he opened the door and told us that Ninong Andy was coming. Nanay and I were in a sort of panic. She was excited to see her old friend and a friend of her husband's. As for me, I was excited to see the person who I only knew from the stories of the people around me.

"Does he have company?" Nanay asked Boyet. She wanted to know if Ninong Andy was with people whom she might have known and were friends of my father.

"Yes. Just one, his wife."

Nanay and I exchanged glances. We were likely thinking the same thing. We prepared a lot of alcoholic drinks, a lot of food to go with the alcoholic drinks, and more food on the living room coffee table. Nanay and I were standing by the doorway, waiting. From afar, I could make out Ninong Andy's figure. It was true what they said about him being tall and having an impressive build. I also noticed his wife, whose height barely reached his shoulder, clutching his arm. As they walked towards us, they started to receive curious looks from the neighbours. Ninong Andy uttered the first word and greeted Nanay.

"Is that you, Elena the Waray-Waray?" he said cheerfully. Tita Belly was right about him being fair-skinned and having soft eyes. I noticed the dimples on both cheeks and partly covered by his thick moustache. He and his wife smiled at us.

"Andy?" was all that Nanay could say as she led the

two inside the house. They were invited to sit before the table. Ninong Andy did not take off the white cloth he wore on his head. His wife's veil was an eye-catching bright yellow. Ninong Andy instantly stared at the San Miguel bottles before him, the pork leg, roasted chicken, and chicharon. Ashamed, I looked away to avoid his gaze. There was an awkward silence.

"I'm sorry, Andy," Nanay said. "I had no idea that..."

"I've been a Muslim for six years, Elena, and I failed to tell everyone," he said. "And this is my wife Khadija."

Nanay extended her hand towards Khadija.

"So, what are we going to do with all of this?" he blurted. Then he burst out laughing. Even Khadija giggled, clutching Nanay's arm.

"My god, what has happened to our life, Andy!" Nanay chuckled. Then all of us gathered around the table exploded in laughter. This was the first time I saw Nanay laugh so heartily, her eyes watering. It was a satisfying moment of sheer joy at seeing her long-lost friend once again. I looked at Ninong Andy, who was still laughing. Maybe they were once like this with Porboy, and this was how close they were to each other. Maybe this was how they were when they were young.

"Your friend's gone, Andy. Porboy is gone." Nanay said this without telling Ninong Andy what he had known for a long time. She said this because I knew they both loved my father. "I hope you have forgiven Porboy."

"I did, Elena. And every day I pray that he forgave me for what I did in Negros."

Nanay was sobbing. More than a decade's worth of grieving seemed all too fleeting.

"We're old now, Elena. I have never forgotten how Porboy introduced you to me when he returned to Bacolod after your wedding. He had you sit alone on a bench in front of the Capitol and then left, so that I could approach you and talk to you. He did not even want to see my shadow, but still he fulfilled our pact to introduce each other to our respective wives and to stand as godfathers of each other's eldest child. You were still pregnant then." Then he looked at me. "Is this Porboy's eldest child?"

I moved closer to Ninong Andy, took his hand, and placed it on my forehead.

"You look exactly like Porboy when he was still a kid in Negros," he told me. I could see he was pleased and at the same time grieved a loss. "No doubt you're his child... Masha' Allah." ♦

Ministop

Jessica, the ugliest girl on the floor, goes to the Ministop alone on her lunch break at three in the morning.

Jessica stares at the glass window of the office building's thirtieth floor not to see how the darkness of the pre-dawn early morning hours has engulfed Manila, but to look at her reflection: her flat nose, thick lips, and the pimple clusters on the left side of her nose, pimples that are, according to her, caused by the lack of sleep and stress from work. Each time she sees the reflection of her face on the glass window, she thinks this: *Beautiful people… they go together*.

Jessica may not have been blessed with beauty, but she can brag about being the top agent on their floor for six consecutive months. A consistent 100% in the Quality Assurance Audit ("I'll make sure that before I end the call I will ask the customer, 'Are you satisfied with my services, sir?', so they will remember me during the Customer Satisfaction Survey"); Best in Close Rate ("My technique is simple: less call time, higher close rate. But in times when sales are low and it's the Blacks calling—their credit card transactions always declining or having disastrous credit ratings—the higher the number of calls, the more chances of a higher close rate"); Best in Sales Margin ("Remember: Americans are not people, but consumers. Even if they have no need for the product and service, you have to create a need for them"); Best in AHT ("My Average Handling Time is low because I avoid fillers, I avoid small talk. I control the call. They need quick actions, more options. Get it?"). Her name, as well as her picture which she always avoids seeing, is constantly posted on the bulletin board on the wall near the office pantry. She keeps avoiding glancing at her picture under the label 'BEST AGENT'. There must be a part of that picture of her face which she can't bear to see directly. No nightshift passes in which the Area Operations Manager is not heard praising her performance on the floor. For Jessica, each day in the office is important to her metrics, to her monthly performance audit as an agent. And for a year, she is able to maintain a spotless record: no absences, no 'No Call No Show', no AWOL, no overbreaks. And when asked about what her secret is for consistently being the floor's top agent, she uses two spiels for her fellow agents:

"Simple: self-discipline and my motto."

"Ha? What's your motto? Share it with us, girl."

"Planning prevents poor performance," says Jessica. On the floor, she's a stickler for the English Only Policy ("How can you master the language if you are not going to practice using it?").

Her fellow agents can only trade knowing looks. "Wow, Jessica, you're really good," they say, in the spirit of civility. But behind her back, they secretly laugh at her because whenever Jessica speaks, she has the tendency to expose her gums to the point that she resembles a fish. She does look like a fish when she talks. And she knows it, knows what the people on the entire floor secretly call her: "shark"—because she does look like a shark. She takes all this in her stride, secure in the fact that she graduated cum laude and is the top agent on the floor. "So what? I'm the best agent on the floor," she says, and adds bitterly: "Beautiful people, they go together and I don't need them."

Jessica has been with the company for almost two years. This is her first job straight out of graduating from the Polytechnic University of the Philippines. Promotion has been offered to her many times by her team leader, by the operations manager, even by HR and the senior operations manager. Her usual response to these offers of promotion is "I'll think about it." Jessica is content with being an agent, with working in front of a monitor and computer all night while wearing a headset connected to an AVAYA.

"You need to get out of your headset, girl," her team leader once said during a coaching session. "You can't be an agent forever."

"I'll think about it, TL. I'm still happy with my job. Imagine, the moment you log out from the AVAYA, that's it. You don't bring anything home with you. Work is over."

Jessica, the ugliest girl on the floor, goes to the Ministop alone on her every lunch break at three in the morning. No situation can prevent her from going to the Ministop. Even when it's raining or the dead of night, she walks through the vacant lot at the side of the Strata Building which she needs to cross to get to Emerald Avenue where the Ministop is located. She doesn't mind the muddy ground and the tall, overgrown weeds on the vacant lot, as long as she gets to the Ministop to buy Kariman, Coke, or any food inside the glass display shelf of the convenience store. Amazingly, she always walks alone when going to the Ministop. It is as if she finds pleasure in passing through the dark and muddy vacant lot.

"Hey, Jessica, why don't you join us later during our 45-minute break?"

"You should. Girl, you're being antisocial. Go with us to the pantry on the 32nd floor."

"All right, but I like the Ministop," is how she declines the invitation of her fellow agents.

One night, as Jessica walks across the vacant lot to reach the Ministop, she notices a shadow. A man is standing, seemingly as if to follow her every move. She is alone in crossing the muddy and dark vacant lot because people who normally pass through the area are too lazy to go to the Ministop and have otherwise elected to stay in the office building in the aftermath of the heavy rain.

She hears him say "pssst." She walks faster, noticing

him do the same to match her pace. The shadow, indeed, belongs to a man. In her haste to get out of the vacant lot, her toe hits a protruding rock. The man catches her by the arm in time, preventing her fall.

"Hi," he says, smiling. Because he has the hoodie of his sweater up, Jessica can't make out his face. He is still holding her arm. His other hand is inside his sweater pocket.

Jessica is speechless, trying to make out the man's face through the dark.

"I know you're from Ambergris. I know a lot of people in Discovery, used to go with them here. I'm sure you don't notice me whenever you pass through there. You always keep your head down." He lets go of Jessica's arm, but his right hand is still inside the pocket of his sweater.

"I'm sorry... I don't know you," Jessica says and continues to walk.

"Wait. I know you're going to Ministop. I always see you there at this hour."

Jessica does not stop walking until she reaches Emerald Avenue. All of the streetlights are blazing. In corners, there are call centre agents from different companies all along the avenue. All of them are smoking by the side of the road. The man is still following her. Eventually, he catches up and is now walking alongside her.

She stops and faces him. Because he has taken off his hoodie, she finally sees his face. He smiles at her. She smiles back. He towers over her and has an impressive build. Although he is wearing a cap (with a Nike insignia at the centre), she can see his face clearly—the small eyes, the thin lips. He is wearing faded jeans and a red T-shirt underneath his sweater.

"I've been seeing you all the time when I cross the parking lot. You are mostly by yourself."

"Really?" Jessica says, pleasantly thrilled. "I don't

remember seeing anyone when I go this way."

"Yes. You, headed for the Ministop here in Emerald. Me, on my way to ADB Avenue, in front of JMT."

"Really? I had no idea we were taking this route through the vacant lot. I mean, I didn't notice you."

"You walk with your head down all the time," he says, grinning. "You should be proud, chin up when walking."

"Anyway, I'm Jessica." She extends her hand, feeling the heat of his palm when they shake. She is mildly unsettled by the fact that he uses his left to shake her hand.

"Let's go to the Ministop."

"Weren't you going to ADB?"

"Ah? Not anymore. I changed my mind because I met you."

Colour drains from Jessica's face. She hides her smile. "So, what do you do at JMT?"

The man averts his gaze, making an effort to avoid looking Jessica in the eye. "Come on, let's get some Kariman at Ministop."

That's their first lunch together.

In the nights that follow, the two keep bumping into each other and ending up at the Ministop. Jessica begins to look forward to her 3:45 a.m. lunch break. There are times when the man waits for her at the other end of the vacant lot at Emerald Avenue.

"Wait, are you from Ambergris in Raffles?"

"What's your favorite Kariman?"

"Pork."

And their conversation will be diverted to the different Kariman flavours available at Ministop.

"By the way, what's the deal with the JMT Building? Why go there?"

"Nothing, I just have a *thing* there..." Then he points at the poster in the counter. "What do you call that?"

"A corn dog."

"Why is it called a corn dog?" he asks, his smile beautiful.

Without fail, Jessica remains quite taken by the beautiful eyes of her newfound 'lunchmate'. And the serenity in his face, too. It shows no trace of exhaustion or lack of sleep, unlike hers whose body midway through the shift already feels like it's been run through a meat grinder. He still wears the same Nike cap.

A week goes by and Jessica has developed a routine of spending her Ministop lunch break with the man.

"Don't you ever get tired of the call centre?" he asks her one time. Between them on the table are fried chicken, rice, and two bottles of Coke.

"Which one? The lack of sleep? I got used to it. In the daytime, I get six hours of sleep."

Sometimes, they talk about work, too.

"And we should thank the stupidity of Americans."

"What? Why?"

"Because if they were intelligent, we wouldn't have our jobs," Jessica explains.

"But they're the ones paying our salaries, right? Therefore, they are the intelligent ones."

In the two weeks of spending time at the Ministop, they have learned to maximise Jessica's 45-minute lunch break. Overbreaks during lunch have been prohibited because of the long queue of calls. The ongoing mutiny of disgruntled soldiers at Oakwood Hotel in Ayala has affected the operation of various call centres around Makati, which means that there are not enough people to handle the volume of incoming calls. It is the first day of the Oakwood Hotel takeover by rebel soldiers protesting against the current government. Several call centres in Makati have been shuttered for the safety of the employees in the event of a shootout between government soldiers and soldiers siding with the leader of the coup d'état. The calls going to the Makati offices have been rerouted to a faraway call centre in Ortigas where Jessica works. The same thing happens during holidays in the United States: Christmas, New Year, Thanksgiving, opening of classes—there are thousands of calls on queue. Bathroom breaks are prohibited. Pressing After Call Work, too, even for a minute just to catch a breath after finishing a call. The atmosphere on the operations floor is like being inside a pressure cooker. Breathing between each call becomes the only source of comfort and rest for agents—and for Jessica, breathing *and* the Ministop lunch break with the man.

"Too many calls!" she says. "My AVAYA is smoking! Super queuing!"

"But why? Christmas is still months away... you said call volumes increase as Christmas nears? And that Americans are not people but consumers."

"Because of the coup d'état in Makati. Many did not show up for work. Offices near Ayala were also closed."

"Gloria's government truly lacks order. It was better during Erap's time."

Jessica bristles at his comment, "No way! I hate Erap. Did you not join EDSA Dos Revolution when Erap was ousted?"

"Joined. It was a party!"

"See, so that's it. We should thank Gloria. Because of her, the number of call centres in the Philippines increased."

"The number of sleepless people also increased," he says, which marks the end of their discussion as Jessica's breaktime is about to end.

When the next monthly performance review of agents on the floor is posted, everyone notices the decline in Jessica's attendance metric from all of her over-lunch violations. She has lost her perfect attendance record. Jessica can't seem to get enough of talking to the man. They've talked about pretty much everything, including the various goods sold at Ministop, soft drink brands, Hollywood films, the major difference between Starbucks and Figaro coffees, the different brands and models of recently released mobile phones. For Jessica, talking to the man at Ministop is the closest she has ever gotten to godly power, to an extremely beautiful creature.

Constantly daydreaming about her 45-minute break at Ministop, she is not always in the proper frame of mind to be talking to customers on the phone. Several times she gets customers to hang up on her because they can't understand what she is saying. Her ideas and explanations are all over the place. One time, a customer berates her for her lack of familiarity with an existing promotion posted on Livewire. And, during the audit, QA chances upon the call where she fails to read a required legal script verbatim or obtain the client's confirmation before processing an order – all because she can't wait to log out and see the man at Ministop.

Jessica, the ugliest girl on the floor, now has a man for company during her treks to the Ministop. She is no longer the best agent on the floor.

Jessica begins fussing about her looks as well. The changes in her have not escaped the attention of her coworkers. She has started to apply foundation, buy lotions and colognes from Watson's, shop at Kamiseta, and avoid wearing denims. When the month's stack ranking list is released, Jessica ends up in 30th place. In the span of a month, Jessica amasses four incident reports from customers, two failures in quality audit, and eight overbreaks. But all seems well for her. She is wearing, after all, her new People Are People blouse, Tyler shoes, and Maldita skirt. Plus, she has something special to look forward to during her 45-minute break at Ministop.

One night as Jessica walks the darkness of the vacant lot, the man calls out to her. He is standing in the part of the lot that is near a construction site. When he approaches her, she has the feeling he has been waiting for her to show up.

"What happened?" she asks the man, who looks quite anxious and is not making eye contact. Jessica can no longer see the usual peacefulness in his face.

"I've been standing here longer than you think, waiting for you."

"Why? What happened?"

"Nothing. I just like being in this vacant lot at night." Once again, he refuses to answer her questions.

"Ha? Why here?"

"Nothing, really. Jessica..."

"What?"

"Nothing." Then he starts crying. Jessica feels mildly embarrassed, worried that someone might walk in on the scene of a man sobbing in front of her. Good thing the place is deserted at this hour. She can't bring herself to pry as she feels they don't really know each other beyond their frequent casual chats. She doesn't know where he's from, or even his name, so asking him to elaborate on his personal problems is out of the question.

"This dark lot, I no longer want to be here, Jessica."

"What do you mean?" Jessica says, confused. "I don't understand what you're saying. You're scaring me."

"I no longer want my job."

"No problem. Let's talk about that in Ministop. Come on, let's go."

The two walk until they get past Emerald Avenue. When they reach the road, the man pauses.

"Why? We have to hurry because I already have a written warning from all the overbreaks."

He holds her hand. She feels the coldness of his palm. The cold travels from his hand to her body like electricity. This is the first time that a man has held her hand, the first time that a man has touched her, touched her in such a way that tingles her most sacred insides.

"I hate my job," he says.

"You don't need to love your job. Who wants to attend to hundreds of calls every night? You can resign if you want to. I can even go with you to get your clearance signed. The clearance you can probably get at Discovery, I don't know. Don't worry, I'll be with you. But be sure you already have a job with another call centre before you submit your resignation."

"You don't understand."

"I do," she says, saddened by the thought of not having anything to look forward to during her Ministop breaks. "Call centres always have high attrition rates. That's normal—to resign from a call centre is normal."

And he finally begins to open up to her. "I'm not from Ambergris, Jessica."

"Okay..."

"I'm not working for any call centre."

Jessica bursts out laughing. "My god! You are working here, in this dark empty space?" she says of the dark and muddy vacant lot.

He is not smiling.

Cool night air wafts in from Emerald Avenue. The two stand under a lamppost, its weak glow shining down on them. He is still holding her hand. He clutches it tightly.

"Aside from call centre work, what other night jobs do you know, Jessica?" he asks shyly.

She takes away her hand. It is as if the cold has reached her chest, her soul. Breathing becomes hard, and the cold might have reached her knees because she feels weak there and just wants to collapse. A few cars have passed by Emerald Avenue. Both of them are not speaking. Jessica thinks, *But I don't really know him. How many people I don't know and talk to everyday. You are just one of those strangers.*

"I'm sorry. Now you know."

"It's okay. No problem. By the way, which Kariman would you like tonight? It's on me again."

While they eat Pork Kariman, Jessica is thinking about how this is the last time she will go to the Ministop. They barely speak, because that's really how goodbyes should be, Jessica thinks. Farewells do not always have to be generously worded. This is her last Kariman, the last time she will see this man.

"Beautiful people, they go together," she whispers to herself as she walks back to the vacant lot leading to the Discovery Centre where she is set to click Auto-in and accept more calls. She laughs secretly at what she has done. The fog is gauzy around her. Sunrise is almost beginning. "Beautiful people, they go together," she keeps mumbling to herself, knowing she will be this month's Best Agent once again. ♦

The Flirt of Rural Tours

The passengers overheard an exchange between a Tagalog and a hunky stranger, both of whom were from Iligan. Because passengers had to endure almost six hours of a tiresome journey from Cagayan de Oro to Davao City, they killed time by eavesdropping—blatantly or in secret—on other people's conversations, as well as by looking outside the window of the Rural Tours Bus and watching a Lito Lapid film on television.

"Your breast looks good." The hunk stared at the pendant worn by the Tagalog.

"Excuse me?"

"That fish on your breast, it's beautiful. May I touch it?"

"Ah, this? I bought it from a Meranaw vendor in Iligan."

"Are you Tagalog, '*Day*?"

"No. From Pasay City. What about you, '*Dong*?"

"From around here. I'm going home to Maramag. You from Iligan?"

"Maybe. You?"

"From Kolambugan. Where you headed?"

"To Davao. For the Holy Week."

"Why? Do you have a boyfriend in Davao?" the man grinned.

"You think we're close enough for you to ask that?" the Tagalog smiled back. "I'm still single."

"I'm single, too. And searching... Wait, where do you work?"

"NGO. Our office is in Manila but we have projects here in Mindanao. You, where do you work and what were you doing in... where was it again?"

"In Kolambugan, in Lanao del Norte. Guess what I do for a living?"

"Constru?"

"What?"

"Sorry. Construction worker? You look like a construction worker."

"I'm a soldier. Do you want a soldier for a boyfriend?"

"Excuse me?"

The hunk was still looking the other man in the eye. The Tagalog noticed for the first time the dimples of the man from Maramag. The hunk had badly sunburnt skin, and his impressive build was obvious in the skintight shirt he was wearing with its faded oversized logo of Coca-Cola.

"Soldiers are said to be sweet lovers."

"I don't want to be a young widow."

Both burst out laughing.

"What places were you able to visit here in Mindanao? You look like you've already travelled all of Mindanao."

"Not really. I haven't been to Western Mindanao and the Sulu Archipelago."

"I bested you. I've already been there. In Maguindanao... in Sulu... in Patikul..."

"What? Nasty name for a place."

"Which one? *Pa-tikul*? You, faggot... But that's a delicious thing to do, especially when you're with someone."

The Tagalog's pulse quickened. It looked like this hunk from Maramag was not only going to remedy the tediousness of this long trip, but he would also address the desires of the flesh. The Tagalog made a mental note about the long stopover in Valencia, where there were several bathroom stalls. Any of those would do.

"Kitanglad is tall..." the Tagalog said to break the silence.

"That's because there's peace and order here in Bukidnon. Just like in Davao... in Iligan... in Cagayan de Oro... Life is good if there's peace and order, right?" he grinned.

The Tagalog thought this was the man taking pride in his job.

They were surveying Kitanglad. Silence. This landmark indicated the Rural Tours Bus's entry into Malaybalay in Bukidnon.

"Have you ever killed someone?"

"Ha?" the hunk from Maramag, who had been to Iligan and Cagayan de Oro, places of 'peace and order', smiled pleasantly.

"You know how to fire a gun?"

"Is that a question? Of course, I'm a soldier. I can fire any type of gun. Do you want me to shoot a load in you in Davao? ... I'll be there during the Holy Week."

They were silent. The Tagalog clenched his hand into a fist. Tightly. He had been working in Mindanao for a long time, and it was true what he had claimed about visiting some parts of the island. And he discovered quite a lot about places that had so-called 'peace and order'—an example of which was the city of Iligan in Lanao del Norte. 'Peace and order' meant there was no Moro rebel, no Muslim rebel.

"I am not going with a man who holds a gun. How far are we to your destination?"

"One more station after Malaybalay. Do you want me to visit you in Pasay City when I'm in Manila?"

"Crazy. You won't find me. And I won't look for you."

"So why don't we meet in Davao next week? You game?"

"Your line of work must be hard. You sound like you've been deprived of someone to talk to for thousands of years."

"I really talk a lot because I have no one to talk to for months at a time. The stories keep piling up. Sorry for being so chatty. But it's a long ride..."

"It's okay. You've been acting like we're close."

"What do you do in your NGO?"

"Human Resources. Boring."

"It's exciting to fight against the enemies of the government."

"Excuse me?"

He moved his mouth close to the Tagalog's ear. The Tagalog could feel the hot breath of the hunk from Maramag. He whispered the next part of the conversation, which the other passengers missed.

"I killed many. More than 20... they were MI... in Barira during Erap's all-out war."

"Ah, is that so? I haven't seen anyone killed violently... is your dick pink?"

Grinning, his mouth still unbearably near the Tagalog's ear, he muttered: "In Davao next week, you'll see..."

And the other passengers failed to hear this intimate transaction designed only for consenting adults.

"What's your number?"

The Tagalog gave his mobile number.

"By the way, I'm Rhon-Rhon..."

"With an H? Jologs is funny."

The hunk from Maramag extended his hand, and the Tagalog gave him his name.

For the remaining hours of the trip, they talked about a lot of things. They agreed to meet in Davao in the week following Holy Week—which was something that the hunk from Maramag believed. Several passengers heard them clearly and witnessed the clash between two starkly different lives and histories.

When the bus reached Maramag, the man got off the bus and waved to the Tagalog. "See you next week... just text." The Tagalog rested his head against the softness of his seat. And he thought about how he would spend Holy Week in Davao alone, bored out of his wits in a city which also had 'peace and order'. He did not give out his real name or his real number. And what bothered him as he watched the houses, trees, mountains – each one with their own set of stories – roll past the window of the moving bus: he felt nothing, not even a hint of regret. ◆

Piety in Wartime

Imo saw how a long bamboo pole was used to fish out corpses from the water. As usual, floating dead bodies were once again collected from the Pasig River by the people of Kuta. From the riverbank, the people of Kuta extended a long bamboo pole to drag the floating bodies to shore. That day, and because there was another clash in the part of the Li District that spanned the places surrounding Laguna de Bay, several dead bodies were found drifting. To watch how the now-lifeless vessels were taken out of the water, Imo and Wanda hid in the tent of one of their neighbours in Kuta.

"Imo, those bodies will be taken to Sanctuario again, no?"

"No doubt! Last night I saw more dead bodies taken from the river. Have you noticed that the ones they bring to Sanctuario are those that don't have any worms or whose stomachs have not ballooned yet from all the water coming in? They only take the bodies with fresh wounds."

Imo was older by two years than Wanda, whose height barely reached Imo's shoulder. The two weren't siblings, but Kuta residents always saw them playing together. Wanda's family was said to be from the Li District, while Imo and his family were from the Xiamen District, which was located at the mouth of the river facing Manila Bay. Like the residents of Kuta, Wanda and Imo were both settlers in the camp. Kuta stood on the ruins of the former Fort Santiago, which had been a Xiamen District park during the pre-war era due to its lush trees and old buildings. These buildings were constructed several hundred years previously before the archipelago became a province of the Beijing Government, which happened during the 'Age of the Hundred-Year Invasion' of the United States Empire. For three out of the five years for which the war was underway, Imo and his family lived in Kuta. Wanda, on the other hand, was an orphan who had strayed into the camp.

"I didn't notice that," said Wanda, in awe of her friend. "You're really smart. Do your mama and papa also tell you what happens to the dead bodies in Sanctuario?"

Imo's parents were active in their Sanctuario duties. They accepted the corpses fished out of the river.

"Each time there's bombing or a clash, or a war vessel is sunk by either the US or Beijing, surely you can expect more bodies to be hauled out from the Pasig River and sent to Sanctuario."

The war between the United States Empire and the Beijing Government had been waging for five years. For eight decades, the Beijing Government had annexed the Philippines as a province, and the terms of their occupation had already expired. Before the Beijing Government was a century-long occupation by the United States. Some eight decades ago when the Empire lost the war to Beijing, a treaty was created between the two superpower nations. The treaty called for Beijing to return the Philippine archipelago to the United States in exchange for eight decades of peace in the Philippines and for the archipelago's natural resources to be left untouched by the war. It had been five years since the Beijing Government refused to return the archipelago and the United States Empire had engaged in repeated attempts to retake one of its Southeast Asian colonies. And throughout these five years, battles raged across the archipelago; people were either displaced or deported so they could survive and move on with their lives. Kuta was one of those places where people settled after fleeing war-torn areas.

Wanda continued to be amazed by Imo's knowledge of how the cadavers were taken from the river and brought to Sanctuario, which had the biggest tent in Kuta. Wanda was baffled by how Imo managed to know more when they were always together gathering old tyres in Pasay in the Xiamen District, entering abandoned buildings in Makati in search of food, walking the Pasig shoreline, riding Merdeka's motorcycle to see Manila, and watching the encounters of soldiers from both warring sides. Wanda imagined Imo passively getting all his information from his parents. Sanctuario had strict rules—whatever happened inside the big tent stayed in the big tent. Imo's parents were frequently seen by Kuta residents coming in and out of the Sanctuario. Imo's mother, in particular, was often seen holding bundles of white cloth, and sometimes a white flag.

"Imo, why don't you ask your Nanay and Tatay what they do with the bodies in Sanctuario? Who are the people there and why can't the kids be there; why are only some Kuta people allowed to enter?"

"Ay! I tried asking Tatay. I only got hell for it. Told me I shouldn't meddle in old people's business. He even said: 'Don't test me, Imo, I can return you to the Central Government with just one click of a button!'"

Thirteen years ago, the Central Government gave Imo to his parents, whose biological children were seized for distribution to other families in different parts of the archipelago as part of the Beijing Government's Comprehensive Family Planning Program for its provinces.

"But there's no government now because of the war?" Wanda said. No parents could be found and assigned to Wanda yet. Because of the war, the operations of all Beijing agencies and services were suspended.

"Yes! We don't have a government yet until we know whose won the war."

"Eh, your father is a fool, he even fools you."

"Mind your language, Wanda, he's still my father according to the law. No wonder the government hasn't given you a family yet," Imo said, knowing the subject was a touchy one for his friend. "And one more thing, Nanay said that sending those dead bodies to Sanctuario was actually for us, for young people."

It never failed to touch Wanda's nerve whenever Imo mentioned her lack of parents. Wanda was in school when an encounter in their district destroyed their complex, and all the houses burned down. She returned home from school to find only the ashes of their house and her parents, also assigned to her by Beijing, missing. Since then, Wanda pretty much went with everyone, wandering in various other Kuta settlements in other districts until an old woman took her in and brought her to the Kuta near the Pasig River. In wartime, the old woman took care of Wanda until the two of them were accepted as settlers of Kuta, which welcomed refugees from different parts of the archipelago. Wanda lived alone, loitering in Kuta and along the Pasig's riverbank when she was not with Imo.

Wanda met Imo when she once crossed Jones Bridge to get to Escolta. Imo was sitting on the bridge's guardrail and watching the river and the floating debris—tyres, tin roof sheets, cars that looked as if a bomb had been dropped on them because they either had massive holes or were split in half, as well as the bodies of those killed in encounters from various parts of the district. Slowly approaching Imo from behind, Wanda aimed to prank him by pushing him towards the Pasig River. As she was about to shove him, a bomb was dropped on an already damaged building in Escolta. The building exploded and flying debris almost hit them. Imo turned abruptly, seeing Wanda positioned to push him into the river, something that many kids enjoyed doing. He hit her in the face until blood gushed out of her nose. Strangely, after that, they were regularly seen at Jones Bridge or running to and fro everywhere, entering Escolta's abandoned buildings to get to Ongpin, where they scavenged items to take home with them to Kuta.

Their friendship further deepened when Wanda's caretaker passed away. The old woman died of cholera in Kuta. People gossiped about how she had been seen drinking water from the Pasig River. Wanda could still remember what happened to the old woman who took care of her: her body ended up at Sanctuario. Wanda cried, with Imo next to her, as the old woman's lifeless body was lifted from her makeshift bed of sacks and cartons. It was still fresh in her mind how Imo's mother instructed the men carrying the corpse to "hurry, before the body becomes stiff!"

As Wanda was sobbing, an old woman from Sanctuario embraced her, trying to offer comfort. "Hay, Wanda, stop crying... don't worry, she died for you. Someday, you will understand everything... they can't take our histories from us because the death of one... preserves our memories." Although Wanda had no idea what she had been told, she could feel the tightness of her embrace and the heat of the old woman's arms clutching her. Wanda wanted to free herself from the embrace, wanted to claim a space for her body. Since then, Wanda had become mindful of preserving the space between her body and those of other people, even with Imo.

"Eh, that's what the old lady told me when they took my old woman's body."

"That was no longer a body, just a corpse. I don't know. But like what Nanay keeps saying, that all those were for us—the corpses—all for us siblings, for the children..." And then Imo told Wanda they had to leave and ride the motorcycle again, which he was able to borrow from Merdeka.

The use of all kinds of motor vehicles was temporarily prohibited all over the archipelago, even aeroplanes because there were several incidents when they were mistaken for attack jets. The motor's noise could invite attacks from outsiders, from enemies. Many people were already killed by mistake; their motorbikes were instantly shot down, the passengers mistaken for enemies. It was only a week ago when two Kuta teenagers on a motorcycle were killed by a hail of bullets from Beijing's soldiers. It disheartened the Kuta community that their number was reduced by two. It put them off further to discover that the bodies were completely burned by the explosion of the motorcycle's gas tank. The corpses were said to be useless and could no longer be taken to Sanctuario.

"Aba! My motorcyle is high-end!" Imo bragged to Wanda as he hurtled down Makati. They heard about relief goods being dropped on the rooftops of old buildings in Makati, and they were eager to get whatever was left of the relief goods since they knew many people, just like them, were rushing to the rooftops to retrieve the food items, household supplies, emergency kits, bottled water, and blankets that the Red Cross had sent. The pair were most interested in the white blankets.

"Eh, but this is not yours, blowhard," Wanda said, referring to Merdeka's motorcycle. Merdeka was Imo's older cousin.

Truth was, Imo did not ask for his cousin's permission to use the motorbike. "Ah, no. Merdeka said he was giving this to me. So it's mine!" he said as he speeded up.

The wind brushing against their faces smelled of gunpowder, burning wood, and rotting human flesh. The war could be in its final stages, or as many assumed it was about to end because the Beijing Government and the United States Empire seemed close to reaching an agreement to just divide the archipelago to the satisfaction of both superpower nations. The delay in laying out the terms of agreement had to do with the unending recount of islands in the Visayas and who got to own them. Imo and Wanda could still hear the distant explosions and guns being fired. The sky was darkening again with smoke from all the buildings that were burning down. The two were nearing Makati, traveling the length of EDSA.

"Merdeka said this motorcycle had a new battery. Is that true?" asked Wanda. "Merdeka's really a survivor, and can live through the war because he can fend for himself. Good at being alone, Imo."

Once again, he heard Wanda's favorite phrase, "Good at being alone."

The war forced the Beijing Government to ration out batteries. But there were black markets in the districts of Li and Xiamen where one could buy car batteries, or trade them for food, clothes, or tarpaulin for tents.

"Yep, brand new. It's supposed to last 20 years."

"You, now where did you get the new battery? You and Merdeka stole it?"

"During the war," Imo replied, curtly. "Tatay said you couldn't own things during the war. You own everything during the war."

"That's not true. Surely someone owns the war."

"Ha? Who?"

"The one who's good at being alone—the stronger one." Wanda laughed, knowing her friend wouldn't get it.

"Tarantado ka, Wanda, you think you're so smart. You just heard that from Merdeka!"

Imo and Merdeka stole the battery three days ago from an abandoned house in a town north of the Xiamen District. Big house. The pair knew the house was owned by a government official. Although the mansion's roof had chipped off and the gate had fallen apart, land and air vehicles were still intact in the yard. As expected, they had no luck finding a battery in the vehicles. They entered the house, and found it empty. The owners likely fled to the Mainland. But Merdeka was familiar with the houses of wealthy Beijing Government members. They were outfitted with hidden basements, where motorbikes, computers, and guns were stored. Merdeka found the strategically concealed tunnel leading to the basement, where a battery was kept among the family's guns, computer, and motorbike. Merdeka kept the newfound motorcycle and decided to give his old one to Imo. He could not, however, pass it on right away because the new motorcycle needed first to be stripped of its monitoring device, which was linked to Beijing's Central Computer. It would take a week for a junk shop in Makati to remove the device.

When Imo and Wanda reached Makati, they parked in front of a building. There were so many people, so they did not expect there would still be any relief goods left. They waited for an hour until the crowd began to thin. Wanda went to the rooftop alone and found it deserted. There were no more relief items left, except for what luck had reserved for them: the one item they wanted to get. Imo gave marching orders to Wanda before she went up the building's rooftop: "The most important thing, and what we need to take home to Kuta, are the white blankets." And there, without fail, were hundreds of white blankets made of canvas cloth.

§

When the pair arrived in Kuta, they carried with them bundles of what looked like a hundred white blankets. Merdeka was there waiting for them at the community's entryway. He was the son of the eldest sibling of Imo's mother. Merdeka's family was among those who had attempted to escape to Vietnam, another Beijing Government province, and drowned as their small boat sank in the South China Sea. Empire drones stationed in Subic mistook the boat for a warship and fired missiles at it. Fate had been kind to Merdeka, who was not on the doomed boat because he was unable to leave the dormitory at the university where he was studying Computer Engineering, and was later included in the Beijing Government's conscription.

"You scamps, where were you?" Merdeka said. Merdeka was angry; Imo could tell from his cousin's thick eyebrows that appeared to join comically into one arc. Merdeka was tall, with Imo only reaching his shoulder level. Imo and Wanda did not say anything, but Merdeka could read them and knew they used his motorcycle to venture outside of Kuta.

"Didn't your parents tell you, Imo, not to ride a motorbike and go outside of Kuta? What if you got hit by a stray bullet? A bomb?"

"Then both of us are dead!" Imo said, his tone venomous as he did not take too well to being embarrassed in front of his friend.

Merdeka slapped him across the face. "You are selfish. If you get killed, who will look after your siblings when the war ends, since your parents are old?" Holding his breath and clenching his hands into fists, he continued: "Maybe it's better if you die. If your bodies get burnt, no one in Kuta will have any use for you. You and Wanda are useless! Useless!" And he pummelled Imo's face with his open palm.

Imo could not defend himself because he was much smaller. The same was true of Wanda, who couldn't help her friend. Merdeka only realised he had gone too far with this violence when he saw Imo's bloodied lips. Blood from Imo's mouth splattered across Merdeka's palm, hand, even his arm. Imo was on the ground, and Wanda was rendered immobile with shock. Merdeka stripped off his shirt and wiped Imo's mouth. Hastily and in a panic, he aggressively wiped away the blood as if Imo's small mouth wound was enough to drain the rest of the blood in his body. After wiping Imo clean, Merdeka sent the pair home to their respective tents and told them not to come out until he returned. Imo and Wanda scurried to follow Merdeka's orders.

When they had both left, Merdeka headed straight to the Pasig River. He stopped to observe the water, the floating things and those brought in by the waves—the dead bodies of soldiers and civilians, dead pets such as dogs and cats. Merdeka tossed into the water the shirt he used to wipe Imo's blood and watched the waves take it away. He washed the dried blood off his hands, still shaken by what he had done. "Tarantado ka talaga, Imo... Tarantado..."

After that incident, Imo and Wanda noticed how much Merdeka had changed. Imo began to notice his cousin becoming quiet and withdrawn. Merdeka also stopped asking him and Wanda to go with him to fetch drinking water for Kuta. To earn money, the three of them used to get drinking water for some of the tents in Kuta. Merdeka drove the motorbike during the early morning hours before sunrise. He had quite a reputation in Kuta as a fast but incredibly vigilant rider, managing to avoid explosions and getting shot at, while steering clear of bandits along EDSA. But in the past few days, Merdeka became moody and did not involve the other two in his water runs.

"Maybe Merdeka just wants to be left alone," Wanda told Imo. "Maybe he thinks he's strong enough."

News reached Kuta about the sinking of five attack boats owned by the Empire and its allies—an indication that the Beijing Government was winning, which meant they would stay in the archipelago. And as expected by everyone in Kuta, including Imo and Wanda, there was another set of dead bodies to be hauled out of the Pasig River. Imo's mother asked for help in getting hold of pieces of white cloth. He spent a day searching for them and came up with nothing.

His mother ultimately asked him for whatever he could find, even if the cloth was a faded blue, green, or yellow—as long as it was not black and especially not red.

Imo's mother had been in a similarly agitated state some time ago, desperately in need of pieces of cloth in a particular colour. It was back when the F-22 Raptors of the United States and Beijing engaged over Manila Bay. The people of Kuta woke up one morning to the thunderous sound of attack jets battling it out across the skies of Manila. Three Empire F-22's chased a Beijing Government F-22 making evasive manoeuvres over Manila Bay, with drones from both sides joining the fight. Everyone in Kuta emerged from their tents to watch. In the end, the lone Beijing fighter jet managed to down two of its enemy planes before taking a fatal hit, the people of Kuta watching from the ground how the doomed plane hit the sea. It was an hour later when news reached Kuta about the pilot of the Beijing plane, that it was someone from Manila, not a Chinese from the Mainland or Hong Kong. The people of Kuta lauded the pilot's courage in downing two Empire planes, which became a hot topic on the radio, television, and online news sites. In Kuta, people honoured the pilot. On the same night, Imo and Wanda, hiding behind a ruined wall along the Pasig River, saw people from Sanctuario fish out floating corpses. To honour the pilot, two dozen bodies were taken from the water and arranged on the riverbank.

"Isn't it because of the pilot's bravery that two dozen bodies are offered to the monster in Sanctuario?" Wanda nervously asked Imo. Wanda knew that a three-headed monster was kept in Sanctuario and it was fed with dead bodies.

"Maybe. What I heard from the other kids in Kuta is that it isn't a monster inside Sanctuario." Not even Imo himself could enter the giant tent, even though his parents were the ones bringing the required white fabric inside.

"Eh, it's just the old ones of Kuta who are allowed to get inside Sanctuario."

"I know," Imo said, then bent closer and whispered: "*They* were the ones eating the bodies of the dead."

Wanda's eyes widened in horror.

"They ate my old woman..." she said, remembering the woman who took care of her. "But, Imo, how come they always say they're doing what they do in Sanctuario for us kids?"

Imo thought hard about Wanda's words, then it hit him. His cousin, at his age, would have likely been granted entrance to Sanctuario. "Merdeka! Merdeka! Merdeka knows!" And the two of them decided to go to Merdeka's tent.

The pair did not instantly announce their presence when they reached Merdeka's tent. They hid at the back of it.

"Imo, what's your cousin doing?" Wanda whispered. Merdeka was outside his tent and kneeling on the ground.

"I don't know. He's digging a hole?"

Merdeka was kneeling and in one hand held a wooden stick to loosen the earth, appearing as if he was in pain from his exertion. Imo and Wanda could see the heaviness in the motion of his back and shoulders, but were still at a loss as to why he was acting that way. Imo wondered if it had something to do with Merdeka's behaviour over the past few days when he kept distancing himself from others and was all too anxious.

Merdeka's entire body almost touched the ground. With the stick, he clumsily tried to sketch something in the earth. His hands seemed stiff, the same delicate and able hands the pair had seen on the computer and motorcycle handlebars. Merdeka struggled in vain to make the stick move and trace something across the ground.

"What's he doing, Imo? What if he got rabies? People were talking about how he got bitten by a street dog in

Binondo yesterday."

"I have no idea. Maybe that's why he's been irritable these past few days. Haven't you noticed?"

Merdeka was still attempting to move his stiff fingers and hands. Then he stopped, took a deep breath and began wailing. He thought he was alone, so he tearfully howled in despair. Frustration ate at him. For the first time, Imo saw his cousin cry like a child. For Wanda, loud sobbing was what he associated with the children she played with, as well as her reaction to the old woman's passing and when her dead body was taken to the large tent.

Imo couldn't take it anymore. He extricated himself from the cloth bundles that concealed his presence and called out to Merdeka.

"What are you doing here?" Merdeka's expression was a mixture of embarrassment and surprise.

"What were you doing just now?" Imo asked, staring at Merdeka's hands.

Merdeka did not say anything. He wanted to explain how he did not wish to be sent to the war and was therefore acting out something he had only seen in Sanctuario—but how could Imo grasp this? Merdeka wanted to be like the creature in the big tent—hidden, protected, and served well for his singular ability. The creature inside Sanctuario was known for his hands. Merdeka tried to replicate that same ability earlier, having convinced himself he could do it as long as he could tame his hands and master the use of the wooden stick. He wanted to share this with Imo, but it would violate the one rule in Kuta: the happenings inside Sanctuario were only for the eyes of those allowed inside the big tent's folds. Violation of this rule was punishable by death, because a breach of such nature would endanger the lives of the people in Kuta. The mere secrecy surrounding the contents of Sanctuario was a clear violation of Central Government laws. It just so happened that the Beijing Government was busy winning a war, so the workings of its colonies were barely monitored and scrutinised. Kuta residents took the protection of Sanctuario seriously because they associated the goings-on in the big tent with their hope for the youth and the next generation.

"What was that you were doing, Merdeka?" Imo asked.

Merdeka got up and gently broke the stick, a resigned expression on his face. "I don't want to fight in the war. I don't want to fight in *their* war." His hands were tightly clenched. Merdeka slowly walked to his tent, without looking back at them.

§

News of Merdeka's departure to join the forces in the war quickly spread across Kuta. The elderly were gratified by this, including Imo's parents who acted as Merdeka's guardians when he was orphaned.

"Imo! Imo!" Wanda excitedly rushed towards Imo, who was standing on the Pasig shoreline and killing time by counting the dead bodies on the water's surface—there were soldiers, women, and children. Sometimes there were animal carcasses, including dogs, carabaos, and horses. All the Pasig River floaters ended up in Manila Bay. Imo had developed a pastime of watching the river's floating dead since Merdeka left whenever Wanda played with girls her age.

"Why? What's the news? The Beijing Government won?"

"No, Imo. Another dead body was hauled out of the river. For sure it's because Merdeka left!"

"Eh, but that happens all the time. I thought you had something new."

"There is!" Wanda with her bluster again.

"Really?"

"While we were playing at the beach earlier, I heard two old people talking, sitting on a car wreck. Probably counting the dead bodies as they floated. I heard one of them mention 'Sanctuario', so I hid behind them because I knew it was going to be about the monster in the big tent. I heard what they said. An old man lives in the Sanctuario, not a monster. The old man has power, Imo! He uses a wooden stick with human hair on one end. He is powerful," said Wanda, and, after looking around to make sure no one could overhear them, muttered close to Imo's ear: "And most of all not encoded by the Central Government as a citizen of Beijing."

Imo was wide-eyed with fright and stunned by his friend's discovery.

"A powerful rebel hides inside Sanctuario," Wanda continued. "Yes, believe me, Imo. That's why the older ones in Kuta do so much to protect the rebel. They don't want the children to know because we might tell people outside of Kuta."

"What's this rebel's power? You said something about a stick?"

"You remember what Merdeka did? Imo, that was it! Merdeka tried to copy the old rebel's power."

Imo began to make the connections. A rebel was protected in Sanctuario by the older residents of Kuta, and this rebel was powerful for not being encoded in the General Citizen's Database of the Central Government.

"Imo, you want to go with me to Sanctuario later tonight after they bring out the dead body for Merdeka?" Wanda said. And while she was speaking, blood dripped from her nose. "What was it, Imo?"

"There's blood on your nose."

Wanda wiped away the blood and went on, "What,

you game for later?"

Imo could not respond immediately because he was worried about his friend's bloodied nose. He imagined Wanda being involved in a brawl.

"Let's get inside Sanctuario."

"Alright. By sunset."

§

The corpse taken from the Pasig River that morning was intended for Merdeka's departure. Carrying bundles of cloth, Imo's mother went inside Sanctuario. Imo and Wanda positioned themselves on the piles of boxes crowding a small tent beside Sanctuario, waiting for the changing of the guards on duty. When it got darker and the hour for the shifting guards to arrive drew closer, the pair readied themselves. As soon as the two guards left to meet up with their replacements for the night, they both slipped quickly inside Sanctuario.

The inside of the big tent was brightly lit with kerosene lamps. The lack of windows made the air inside Sanctuario stiflingly hot and dense. The stench of putrefaction was suffocating; dead bodies, drained of their blood, were stacked to one side. To shield themselves from view, the two crouched behind a huge jar. They saw Imo's parents seated before the elder. They followed the motion of the elder's hands: the motion mirrored a series of intricate dance movements atop a white cloth. They saw that the old man indeed wielded a wooden stick as a wand. Imo's mother was speaking to the elder, whose hands still continued to move. Imo looked at his hands, imagining how many years it would take for him to learn the elder's hand motions. They were in awe of the stick's movement across the cloth. They also noticed the human hair strands on one end of the stick. In front of the kneeling elder was a white cloth, and he gently dipped one end of the stick into a blood-filled basin. Silently, the two watched as Imo's mother continued to speak to the elder going through the motions of his ritual.

The cloth, now almost completely bloodstained, began to lift as the level of blood collected in the basin rose.

"Merdeka will be pleased when he comes back!" said Imo's mother.

"That is—if he manages to come back alive," Imo's father replied. "And if he doesn't return, no doubt your nephew is a hero. We'll pass this on to Imo, so his sons will know about Merdeka. This war is almost over."

"We've been living like this for five years," she said. "It was said on the news that Beijing has already agreed to divide the islands in the archipelago, with some of them given to the Empire. I feel, too, that this war is almost over. Hope they'll come to an agreement soon. So we can lead normal lives, peaceful lives like before."

The elder did not join the conversation. He continued to do what he was tasked with, smiling occasionally but still hard at work. He took a break and paused whenever Imo's mother talked, or when he touched his long beard. Sometimes, Imo's father massaged the old man's hands.

It was already morning when Imo and Wanda emerged from the Sanctuario. When the dead bodies, drained of their blood, were carried out of the tent, Imo's parents followed. The tired old man had gone to sleep, and the new set of guards arrived.

"Imo, I need to go home for now. I have a headache. My belly aches, too," said Wanda.

As they went their separate ways, Imo called her back, wiping the blood off her nose. He noticed the blood clots in Wanda's nosebleed.

"You need to stay away from Wanda," his mother reminded him as she arranged the bundles of white cloth whose true purpose Imo had finally uncovered. This comment, however, baffled him. Imo said nothing, just bowing his head and walking out of their tent. As he neared the tent's opening, his mother kept talking, probably recognising Imo's disagreement. "Don't be too hard-headed. Many people saw Wanda drinking water from the Pasig. We can't afford an epidemic and the spread of diseases... what with this war going on."

Imo was startled, but he did not look back at his mother.

"Imo! You have a family. Wanda has none! She's used to being alone!"

His mother was right about Wanda. It was noon when Imo drove Merdeka's old motorcycle and spotted Wanda holding a pail under the Jones Bridge. Once again, she was alone. Although they were almost inseparable, Imo noticed there were times when Wanda would rather be by herself. Wanda was walking towards the Pasig riverbank. She knew the water was not fit for drinking because it had long been rumoured as the cause of the epidemic in Kuta. Imo hid behind the ruins of a building and observed Wanda, who didn't use her pail to get water but for collecting the shrapnel, cans, and other knick-knacks scattered on the shore. Imo felt a twinge of shame for suspecting his friend, and briefly thought of his mother who he figured had lied to him. He was about to call out to Wanda when he saw her kneel and lean close to the water as if to kiss the black river water. She scooped the water with her hand and drank. Imo gunned his motorbike in Wanda's direction. She turned, surprised by her friend's arrival.

Imo slapped her. Wanda cried, her lips bloodied from the blows. She ditched her pail and ran away without looking back.

Days passed, and Imo was still shaken by the incident. He stayed inside their tent. In his dreams, he saw Wanda's death. His mother kept asking him what was wrong, whether he was physically unwell or if there was something in particular that bothered him, all of which were met by Imo's silence. Like Merdeka before him, he became fidgety and withdrawn.

As he slept one night inside their tent, with his parents tending to their Sanctuario duties, Imo was awakened by Wanda's voice. He did not respond. Wanda persisted, coughing occasionally. Imo was torn between his desire to see and reconcile with Wanda while dreading the premonition of her death. He did not know whether it was death itself that he feared, or losing his friend.

"Imo, wake up, let's play! Imo, are you there?" Wanda said over and over.

To keep Wanda from intruding on his self-imposed solitude, Imo covered his ears with pieces of cloth that his mother collected. He left his ears covered until sleep claimed him. As the sound of distant shooting slowly abated, likely another one in their district that had something to do with the war between the two superpowers, Wanda's voice also became just as inconsequential as white noise.

Imo lulled himself to believe in Wanda's unique ability to fend for herself. Unlike himself, who feared abandonment and the loss of a friend. *Wanda is really selfish*, he thought, and fell asleep.

Wanda's dead body was discovered the next morning at the side of a tent near Imo's. As soon as Imo and his parents woke up from the outcry of the crowd around the lifeless Wanda, his mother got up with a startle as if to steel herself for a fight for the possession of the child's body. Carrying a basin, Imo's father accompanied her. Imo had a hard time wrapping his head around the fact that Wanda was dead when it was just last night that she had hollered out for him to play. He sat in a corner, folded his legs and placed his head on his knees, trying not to cry while replaying in his mind his good times with Wanda.

His parents returned an hour later, and his mother frantically searched for a white cloth or any fabric whose colour was fading. He kept his questions to himself, knowing already the answers to them. No doubt Wanda's body was destined for Sanctuario, to the old man with enchanted hands. Her blood would be drained, the body thrown into the Pasig River to join the other floating dead, the broken things like cars and bicycles and animal carcasses.

That same night, Imo slipped inside Sanctuario with the exact same manoeuvre he and Wanda had used some time ago. He knew Wanda's body was still inside the big tent because no one from Sanctuario had gone to the Pasig River yet to dispose of a body.

This time the old man was alone inside Sanctuario. Wanda's body was also there, her skin wrinkled up and blue. The body was placed on a plank, ready for hauling out for disposal in the river.

Imo stationed himself to hide behind bunches of cloth, witnessing once again the old man's rare magic: the movement of his hands as well as the use of a wand dunked in blood, one of its ends placed in contact with a piece of cloth—the same thing that Merdeka did.

Wanda and Imo were the only children in Kuta who witnessed what went on inside Sanctuario. Protecting a person not registered in the Central Government Database, as well as maintaining the secrecy in support of the old man's activities in Sanctuario, was strictly prohibited by the government. Imo knew this long before the war started. He learned it in school. All activities conducted without the knowledge of the Beijing Government were deemed seditious.

The old man finally noticed Imo's shadow. He put down the stick. "Show yourself, whoever you are," he said, softly, which rattled Imo. The old man repeated his order, and Imo had no choice but to reveal his presence. His knees weak with fright, Imo approached the old man whose thick beard and thin lips did not escape the young man's scrutiny. Imo avoided looking the old man in the eye, although there was no anger in his gaze, only judgment. He gestured for Imo to sit down. "Why are you here, child?"

"Wanda is my friend."

"You are Imo? So you are Imo! I know many of you in Kuta, just not your faces."

Imo was confused.

"Wanda is meant for you," the old man said, smiling.

"For me?"

"Yes. Because she had no relatives and you were the person closest to her—she was for you." The old man could see Imo was confused, so he continued. "Ay! If only you knew how your mother fought like hell for Wanda's body."

The old man signalled for Imo to come closer and then grabbed his wand. He dipped one end in Wanda's blood for use as ink in drawing straight lines on the cloth. Lots of lines: some diagonal, others vertical, circular, and parallel. Imo watched with interest the motion of the old man's hands as he performed the ritual, until he saw his name appear on the cloth.

"That's my name! My name!"

"Yes, Imo, that's your name in our language. You probably haven't seen your name outside of it being typed and shown on a computer monitor and written using particular alphabets—the alphabet and technology of those who invaded us."

"Are you a rebel?" Imo finally had the resolve to ask the old man about his identity, knowing full well that it was illegal to write one's name in the alphabet of an old language often used only by rebels.

"My work is for the history of every person, of every important event in a person's life. I use my hands to impart onto the cloth every event and people's important experiences so that the next generation will know their ancestors. They will know their origins."

"How old are you?"

"I am old. I've been here since the United States Empire occupied this archipelago."

"You are that old? You've seen the 'Age of the Hundred-Year Invasion'?"

The old man laughed out loud. "That's what the Beijing Government said—that the invasion was brought on by the Empire... that's their version of our history. There's a lot you don't know."

"But it was true they occupied the archipelago for a very long time. The Beijing Government came to save us. Now they want to invade us again and that is why there's a war."

"Refresh your history, Imo. The archipelago's history. During the time of the United States Empire, we were free. We could speak out, speak up, express our thoughts. What I'm doing now, I was able to do during the Empire's time."

"That's not true. It was the Beijing Government that defended us. That's history."

"There is such a thing as real history. But under Beijing, there's only an 'official history'. It's the Empire that will liberate us. You just need to open your eyes to the truth. Can you do what I'm doing?"

Imo was silent for a moment, perplexed by the old man's talk about the two kinds of history.

"The Empire's legacy was this: the freedom to determine our history, our future."

Imo recalled his parents describing schools all over the archipelago. When he came of age, he went to school where he had to use a computer and keypad. All messages and letters had to be transmitted via email. Everything had to be on the computer, in digitised form and accessible through the internet so that the Central Government could read and review the writings. "That legacy, the Central Government forbids that."

"Yes, just try not to get caught." The old man grinned. "Look at it this way, Imo: Wanda died, not her memory. Time will come for the next generation, and they will know that at one point, there was a Wanda—not an 'official Wanda' of the Beijing Government. They'll never forget, especially your future grandchildren, that you and Wanda were friends." The old man took hold of his wand again and acted as if to go back to the task at hand, a way to communicate to Imo that he had to leave as he had taken up a lot of the old man's precious time. "This won't be erased, Imo. The Central Government will never own this. Never."

§

In the following days, the old man's words haunted Imo. He no longer had a friend but was left with the promise of the old man's magic: that it could triumph over death. He sat on a rock on the Pasig riverside, watching the floating dead and listening to the faraway sound of explosions and guns being fired. There was fighting outside their district again. Then all at once and very abruptly, the shooting stopped. The explosions, too. The silence was new to him. For the past two months, all he heard were the intermittent sounds of firearms and bombs. People came out of their tents, curious about the sudden silence. An aircraft zipped past overhead, one aircraft followed by another until there were almost a thousand of them blanketing the sky, which looked bloodstained by all of the red fighter jets of Beijing.

The people of Kuta rejoiced, realising that Beijing had

won; it won, defending the archipelago—and there would be peace again. The people of Kuta only wanted peace and a return to normalcy, whatever normalcy meant. People could almost dance for joy over this latest development. Imo stayed where he was, thinking just what Wanda would have thought if she was still among them: there would be another dead body taken from the river to commemorate this event. Lots of dead bodies would grace this victory. Imo stretched his legs and walked close to the waterline. He knelt and scooped up water with his palm. He stared at the water he collected in his hand as if to acknowledge its existence and then quickly slurped it. He felt the water down his throat. He looked at his hands, now empty, and realised he would never be able to perform the old man's magic—and he had no intention of ever doing it. Not out of a desire to obey the laws of the Beijing Government and return to a life with a semblance of normalcy, but because he wanted to free himself from a particular kind of loneliness, the same loneliness that engulfed Merdeka. Imo had not understood it then. Now he forced himself to understand: happiness was not about being free, happiness was in fighting back, in the struggle—freedom could only be found in the place where Wanda was now, in being alone. Imo cried in this moment of self-discovery. He smiled. A smile he still wore when he returned to Kuta and mingled with the celebrating crowd. ♦

Is There Rush Hour in a Third World Country?

"Life here sucks, Choning, I told you earlier we should have taken the FX."

"Asus-asus! Your noise is bothering the passengers," Choning said, holding tightly to the cold metal of the passenger railing.

"It wasn't like this back home. I told you this is how it is in Manila. I warned you..."

"Shut up, Elsa!"

The driver opened the door as soon as the bus stopped at the corner of EDSA and Quezon Avenue. Commuters entered hurriedly in droves, driving Elsa and Choning to the back of the bus. With every stop for new passengers, the old ones were forced to move further back. This was how Elsa and Choning ended up at the back of the bus.

Some of the passengers were visibly irked, while some had choice remarks for the bus conductor and driver.

"Choning, do you know where we're going?"

"Of course. In front of the Quiapo Church. Blue and red stripes on a white T-shirt, jeans, rubber shoes. I am scared... this is my first time... Never mind! What happens will happen!"

"Make sure something good comes out of this escapade of yours, Choning. What a shame to have to waste our Friday day off." Elsa was wary of ending up frittering away the rest day that their employer only allowed once a week. "Mrs. might not allow us to go out next time."

"Don't worry. I made sure Arnie would come."

When the bus stopped at Delta, where their Quezon Avenue route met the long highway stretches of Timog and West Avenues, several passengers got out. But twice the number of alighting passengers entered the bus. The conductor kept welcoming more commuters. The bus started to run slowly, the interior becoming stiflingly hot because the air conditioner could not keep up. "Please do something about the aircon," one of the passengers screamed. The driver paid him no heed and continued to drive the length of Quezon Avenue.

"My legs feel numb."

"Hay! Be patient, Elsa, this is really how it is in Manila."

Elsa and Choning had been standing in the cramped bus for at least an hour and a half. And each time a passenger tried to get off the bus, pushing and pulling became unavoidable. Anyone from the back of the bus would have to navigate the impossibly tight space in order to get off.

"So what was your agreement with Arnulfo?"

"What 'Arnulfo'? I told you to call him Arnie." Elsa smiled at the mention of Arnie's name.

"Oh, why are you smiling, Elsa?"

"Arnie's good looking, isn't he?" Then Elsa suddenly thought of the danger. "Choning, be careful. That man is from Manila."

"So what are you saying? You think I don't know that, gaga? Just because I'm from Negros doesn't mean I won't be able to tell when someone's lying to me. This is my first 'eyeball'. And I'm having second thoughts. I don't even know what Arnie looks like... what happens will happen!"

"Where on earth did you find that Arnie of yours?"

"My textmate."

"How did you get his number?"

"Excuse me, it was Drigo, Mrs. Tan's guard, who gave my number to Arnie. It wasn't me who asked for his number."

There was a commotion at the front of the bus. The conductor and a female passenger were arguing. The woman was wearing a uniform and full makeup, shining with too much jewellery.

"If you have so many complaints, why don't you just get a taxi?"

"This rude asshole. No wonder you ended up that way. With a nicer attitude, you could have improved your station in life." She looked around, hoping for others to agree with her. "Your bus is too hot, and you still won't stop letting on passengers."

"But that's just how it is, Mrs. If you don't like the tight quarters of your public commute, then get off the bus. Here, that's your fare. You're not the only passenger in the world. You should be thankful you even got a ride in the first place. You could have been stranded."

The woman stopped complaining moments after the bus rounded a few corners, realising she had no choice and that getting off this bus would translate into not getting a seat in any of the fully packed buses, FX vans, and jeepneys plying the Quezon Avenue route.

"How old did he say he was?"

"30."

Elsa didn't hear Choning's response because the bus driver honked at a man crossing despite the green light. She asked again in Bisaya, "How old?"

"30! Are you deaf?"

Elsa was wide-eyed with amazement. "And he's not married or anything? Oh, no, Choning, there are lots like that here in Manila."

"He's not married. It would be obvious to me if he were. He texted me once that I was his first girlfriend."

"You're already his girlfriend?" Elsa's voice was so loud that it drew the attention of several passengers, though she was aware many had been listening to their conversation. She even caught some of them grinning at their exchange. Elsa was mildly embarrassed. "Good for you, Choning. Me, I've never had any suitor."

"Of course, I'm Choning."

"Aren't you scared he will ask you to marry him?"

"Honestly, that worries me. Maybe that's why he asked me to meet him at a church," she joked.

By the time the bus rounded the corner of Roosevelt Avenue, the traffic slowed to a crawl. The passengers erupted from a combination of annoyance, exhaustion, and boredom. The air conditioner eventually became useless against the rising temperature inside the bus.

Once again, the two were pushed even further towards the end of the vehicle as another batch of passengers came on. Choning's legs felt numb.

"Elsa, tell that man over there, the one wearing Ray-Bans... tell him to give up his seat for one of us. We're women, anyway."

"Ay! No, I can't, Choning. Too embarrassing."

"Come on... he's a big guy. Bigger than the two of us. My legs are going to give up on me."

Elsa could no longer resist Choning's provocation. She came up to the Ray-Bans-wearing man. What worried Elsa was the mortifying prospect of being turned down.

"Ah, mister," Elsa greeted. "May we have your seat? We're women."

The man turned to face her. His expression was blank, his eyes concealed by the dark glasses. They stared at each other for what felt like a long time. There was a throbbing in Elsa's chest. She dreaded being told off. She felt her knees weaken when she noticed the tight knot on the man's brow.

"We are women. May we have your seat?" Elsa repeated.

The man's unreadable expression didn't change. Elsa wasn't sure whether he was really looking at her because she couldn't see his eyes through the Ray-Bans.

"Did you use your pussy for bus fare?" he said.

Elsa went pale and turned her back on the man, never facing in his direction again.

The conductor approached them. "Oh, why are you paying just now when you're from Fairview? Putcha, if an inspector happened to get in here, he'd know I didn't collect your fare yet. I could lose my job because of the two of you, miss. It's hard to find a job these days." The whole time the conductor was talking, he was looking at the roll of bus tickets.

Choning handed over their fare, moved by the bus conductor's words. She understood where he was coming from. If an inspector discovered they still hadn't paid, it would be the conductor's ass on the line. "Two for Quiapo. From Fairview," Choning said, handing over a 500 peso bill. They just got their half-month salary, so they hadn't had a chance to get the money broken down into smaller denominations.

"You don't have change?"

"None," Elsa said. "Our money is in big bills."

"Next time, pay with change in the morning," the conductor said while looking at the money he was counting, his annoyance showing.

"It's already nine. It is no longer *morning*." Elsa quipped, fully resolved to never again lose an argument with anyone on the bus. After that humiliating run-in with the man in Ray-Bans, she couldn't stomach another with the conductor. "We already have a hard time finding a way to pay you. Don't make finding change for the bus fare part of our problem."

He stared at her and wordlessly held out the change. After turning his back on the two women, he muttered with disgust: "Putang inang helpers."

Several passengers giggled at the conductor's comment.

"What did you just say?" Elsa said, hearing only part of the conductor's retort. Based on the other passengers' reaction, she knew it was meant to humiliate her. "Patay-gutom."

That took everyone's breath away. Everyone was

silent. 'Patay-gutom': an expression of contempt towards the poor who had to eat voraciously when presented with food. The conductor heard it and walked back towards Elsa who tilted her face up in a stern challenge.

"What did you say?" he asked, emphasising every word.

"You are patay-gutom," she said, her voice shaky and her hands clenched into fists. She had been called a 'helper' by the conductor and was ridiculed by some passengers. She thought she was finally in the position to avenge herself from all the insults. "And you will die as a conductor."

The conductor raised his hand, poised to backhand Elsa when the passengers yelled at him, "She's a woman. Don't stoop to her level." He came to his senses and returned to the front of the bus.

Elsa burst out crying. Choning embraced her.

"Putang ina, Choning, this is your fault. We should have stayed in the house. We could have avoided all these insults."

The number of passengers inside the bus had thinned as the vehicle passed the final stretches of Roosevelt Avenue, but Elsa and Choning were still unable to find a seat because their fellow standing passengers were quicker to snatch up the vacant seats. It was as if the scene with Elsa and the conductor hadn't happened. There was music: songs by the Backstreet Boys played at a high volume. Choning and Elsa's shirts were drenched in sweat. The woman who complained earlier about the heat was quietly fanning herself, her expression dour.

To occupy themselves, the passengers went back to talking amongst themselves. Choning and Elsa circled back to the subject of meeting Arnulfo.

"I don't know, man, this will be the last time," the Ray-Bans-wearing man said.

"It would be a shame to miss out on the opportunity,"

another man seconded. "Putang ina, especially now they are destroying Erap in Malacañang…"

"That's just how it is, man, they hate Erap who is helping the poor. The Philippines is hopeless."

You made the right decision to return to the ship."

"After this last run, I'll buy an FX and drive it as a passenger van. Working on a ship is hard. You're in the sea for months at a time. The waves are taller than the buildings in Makati. One time I was in a tanker that had an accident. A chain snapped as it was pulled by a Pinoy crew. The chain was bigger than a fist, and it hit his ribs. His ribs cracked. Good thing that the company paid—"

"The Pinoy crew?"

"No. The broken ribs."

They laughed.

"It's hard working for an ocean liner," the Ray-Bans-wearing man repeated. "Terribly boring, too, because you don't see any stretch of land for months."

"I guess you're right. Plus you'll miss your family."

"Especially the wife," the Ray-Bans-wearing man said, grinning. "My dick was sore having to jack off all the time in the cabin."

They traded knowing smiles. Choning heard them and turned in their direction, looking at the man in Ray-Bans, his eyes still concealed from view.

"Choning, UST is really beautiful, no?" Elsa said. "I had the chance to go inside once when I was waiting for Veronica. I sat on the grass, looking at the handsome students."

"If I went with Tita Badet, I could have been in the university, right?" Elsa said, regretting the time when she refused her aunt's invitation to live with them and study in Manila.

"Ay sus! Look at what happened to Badet's daughter who finished Commerce and ended up as a domestic helper

137

in Hong Kong."

"I'm wondering what Arnulfo looks like," Elsa said, in an attempt to change the topic of their conversation.

"I told you, it's Arnie."

Many passengers got off the bus at the corner of Morayta, the closest way out to España Boulevard, which spanned the University Belt where several universities and colleges were located. Vacant seats were finally available for Elsa and Choning, who bemoaned getting their seats at this point when they were already close to their destination. Still, they were thankful for the comfort as their otherwise ten-minute walk from Morayta to Quiapo became a 30-minute bus ride because of traffic.

"Is Arnie good looking?"

"I don't know. I haven't seen him yet."

"You haven't seen his face? You're not friends on Friendster?"

"No. I want our *eyeballs* to have a thrill."

"Choning, what you're doing is dangerous. You don't know what he looks like and yet he's already your boyfriend? What if that Arnie of yours is a bad man?"

"Hay! Just stop. We've been texting for more than three months. And I'm sure: he's not married."

"What if he looks just like Erap?"

"At least he's rich."

"What if he makes you his mistress?"

"Well, if he's as rich as Erap, then why not?"

"Tonto! Gaga! He could be a drunk."

"Is there any man who isn't a drunk? Gambler?"

"I hope you're selective with the kind of man you invite into your life—is that possible?"

"Just stop. You're the one who's choosy with men. See, Elsa, you still don't have a boyfriend. How are you going to find a husband?"

"What happens will happen. I think I'll just go to Germany."

"Gaga! So who will take care of you when you are older? Don't tell me you're expecting me to look after you. If you ever run to me for that, I'll smack you. You need to get yourself a man."

"I will earn money in Germany. You'll never know, maybe I'll find a husband in Germany. Aba! Then I will be married abroad!"

The bus still inched its way through the traffic sprawl. The traffic became packed towards the Quiapo Church. Elsa kept glancing outside the window. She saw the old buildings, people brisk-walking, people walking aimlessly, roads that stayed wet and littered with garbage. This was her first time to walk the grounds of Quiapo. With all the times she had been in Manila and passing through Quiapo, she was inside her boss's car. Now would be her first time to see the Black Nazarene inside Quiapo Church.

"Melba got lucky, no?" Choning said.

"You're right, Choning. I envy Melba," Elsa said, staring outside the bus. "As for me... when will I ever get to travel to other countries?"

"Collect experiences. Is that what Melba said? You've only been with Mrs. for a few months."

"Is there really a need to study that, Choning? Being a housemaid?"

"Of course. If your boss abroad is satisfied with your work, you'll receive a salary increase and your agency will get paid so you become a direct hire, not contracted through them. That's what happened to Melba."

"Really?"

"Have you heard Sandra's story?"

"Sandra from Mrs. Chan?"

"Gaga, no, the one from Mrs. De Leon." Choning

turned to her cellphone because she just received a message. She read the text, smiling pleasantly. Arnie said he was waiting for her at their meeting place in Quiapo.

"So what happened to Sandra?"

"She worked in Macau and then her boss liked her work. There! The agency was paid and when her boss, a Portuguese family, went to the US... Hay! They took that gaga with them."

Elsa was silent, looking outside the bus. She saw many people waiting for whatever available mode of public transportation. Chasing each other. Roughly jostling for space. She also saw old buildings along the side of the road. She looked back to see the long line of vehicles behind their bus. *Good for Melba. Good for Sandra. When will I ever get to Macau, Riyadh, or America? When?*

The two women alighted in front of the Quiapo Church. Choning couldn't walk straight, wearing stiletto heels she had borrowed from a friend, another housemaid working for their next-door neighbour. Choning led Elsa inside the church. She was supposed to meet Arnie there, by the statue of the Black Nazarene.

The doorway of the church was crowded by tables upon tables which vendors used for their root cuttings, dried leaves, dead insects (likely dried for many days), medicinal plants, rosaries, and necklaces (for fighting curses and supernatural creatures). Around the side of the church were fortune tellers. The floor was muddy because the people who visited the church had been to the public market, Binondo, or the wet streets of Manila. Elsa took in the view while Choning was busy looking for her Arnie.

The two women waited next to the statue of the Black Nazarene, staving off boredom by looking at the people entering the church.

"Elsa?" Choning said. "What if he asks me to marry

him?"

Elsa had no idea what to say to her friend. *What if, Choning? I don't know the answer. What happens will happen.* She took her hands and said gently, "Hay! Choning, you can always say no. No skin off your back if you say no, right?"

They heard someone from the church door call out Choning's name.

Both of them could hear the man call out to them. They were still holding hands, facing each other. The voice went on: "Choning! Choning!" And they did not move, appearing as if they had no plans to turn and face the direction where the voice was coming from. It looked as if they were no longer interested to turn and look at the source of the voice. ♦

Two Missing Children

Two children went missing, and nobody knew where they came from. And because nobody knew where they came from, the people of Sebastian did not know how to get the two kids, a boy and a girl, back to their parents. It was a public market vendor in Sebastian who had first spotted the children; they were naked and holding each other's hands. "Those kids were white and shiny!" said the vendor when she saw them walk past the table of her stall. She described their skin as white, white as snow. And because they had no clothes on when they walked into the public market, they stood out in the crowd.

The children roamed the town for days. Their nudity attracted attention, and there seemed to be no end in sight for their long walk. Villagers estimated the girl's age to be eight years old, the boy around nine or ten. According to the city's municipal mayor, who was educated in Manila, the kids had American parents. But many people contradicted the mayor's account, including and most especially his political rival who trailed behind him in the polls.

Marquez, who had lost to the incumbent mayor in the recent election, said that the children could not possibly have American parents because that meant they had privileged ancestry. Marquez went on, crowing about his stint in the United States, where Americans were touted to not forsake their children because children were considered to be their nation's hope. This was the point when Marquez drew criticisms, especially criticisms encouraged by Maning, the renowned village philosopher.

Maning said that Marquez's logic would have shown there was no truth in the claim that American children were not left to fend for themselves because they were the 'hope of their nation'. According to Maning, Rizal, a Filipino, was the source of the idea that children were the 'hope of their nation'. Americans wouldn't heed Rizal because he was not one of them. Marquez bristled at how Maning's counterclaim made him look like a liar and someone only pretending to be knowledgeable about things.

When news of the former politician's angry reaction reached the philosopher, it restored his confidence in sharing more of his perspectives on the issue. Maning headed to the public market and preached to passersby. He regaled them with Marquez's lies and pro-American stances on various issues. This angered Marquez, who happened to pass the public market himself while Maning was talking to people. Many people saw how the former politician stood still, the fury in his tightly clenched fist, facing the sermonising philosopher. "Oh no, there's that deadly threat in Marquez's eyes... Maning should back off," said those who saw what unfolded on that fateful day.

Three days passed, and fishermen found Maning's corpse floating near the bank of the Ragasa River. The philosopher's tongue had been severed. Marquez was never seen again in Sebastian. Villagers believed, with the urging of the incumbent mayor, that it was Marquez who committed the horrific crime.

The two missing children were seen once again a few days after Maning's burial. They still had no clothes on. Passing in front of the Saint Francis of Assisi Church, the children finally caught the attention of the priest, who was appalled by their deplorable condition. *Who were the parents of these kids?* The priest blamed whoever brought the children into this world.

The kids could not speak, the priest revealed when asked by the devotees of Saint Francis of Assisi, the patron saint of Sebastian. The priest prepared clothes for them. For the girl, a pink dress to make her look like a doll. Seeing the girl's green eyes for the first time, he said, "Jackpot! The boy's eyes might also be green." So, he checked the boy's eyes and was instantly disappointed to discover that they were not green but black. The priest continued to inspect the boy.

The one thing the most fanatical rumourmongers of Sebastian had trouble believing was the account of that one drifter who spent an inordinate amount of time loitering around the church front steps. The drifter claimed that when the two kids finally emerged from the church, the boy still had no clothes on, and that he remained naked when he walked out with the girl. The bit about the two kids having different eye colours, and the speculation that they could not possibly be siblings, also reached the gossipers.

It was a dispiriting Sunday, and no mass seemed to be forthcoming. The pews were already filled with people waiting for over an hour, and yet the priest was nowhere to be found. People ended up killing time by rehashing the hot topic involving the two kids.

There was no Sunday mass that morning. By mid-afternoon, two altar boys discovered the priest in his room, dead, the body already cold and stiff. News of the priest's death and the circumstances surrounding it travelled fast around the village. The priest was found naked from the waist down. His right hand still clutched his penis, while his left was balled into a fist and pressed hard against his chest. People hearing about this detail made the sign of the cross, while drunks and loiterers responded to it by laughing heartily. Everyone, rubberneckers and casual observers alike, knew that the priest died in the throes of sexual ecstasy.

But cops did not take things at face value. The two children were the last people seen in the company of the priest, so the search for them intensified. There were talks that hinted at the kids' parents hiding the two children in another town after getting wind of an ongoing search for them in Sebastian. The children's escape became a major point of contention, as well as the heinous crime they supposedly committed. Manila press people arrived, and everyone expected that this incident in Sebastian would blow up to become a national issue.

The Chinese businessman Be Ho Tay, upon hearing the news, scratched his chin. Be Ho Tay, owner of the biggest taho and hopia store in Binondo, pored over various aspects of the news. He decided to go to Sebastian, taking with him five labourers from his rice warehouse. "I will find those kids," he said to himself, "I will profit from them!" He wasted no time and commissioned three newsmen in Manila to make up stories about the kids. The first newsman he instructed to weave a story portraying the kids as extraterrestrials, while the other—a famous tabloid columnist—was told to write about how the children were the spawn of the Devil. The third newsman, who had just graduated from college and needed the money as he was a breadwinner sending his siblings to school, was told to say the kids were nature spirits, *nuno sa punso*, enchanted dwarves living in a mound.

"We need the media," Be Ho Tay smilingly told his labourers. Among the trio he paid to concoct stories, the first one, who wrote about the children as visitors from another planet, received the most traction from the masses, the children's strange appearances helping to solidify the impression that they were not of this world.

"Not all Martians look like E.T.," said a young man in an interview at a Malate rave party. The young man was said to be the son of a well-known businessman in Manila, and he was supposedly an 'expert' on all things alien and extraterrestrial. He said he had read a story in a Manila newspaper about it.

The spreading narrative about the children frightened

the people of Sebastian, who began refusing to leave their homes lest the children would abduct them. People from Manila arrived in droves. There were even tourists from faraway lands, all eager to see the two children reportedly roaming the town of Sebastian.

Months passed, and still there were no sightings of the children. They were never seen again walking the fields and playing in barns. Still, tourists kept coming. Be Ho Tay profited so well that he was able to put up a restaurant, a movie house, and a motel; business was booming in Sebastian.

After a year, Malacañang got wind of the news and the president had a flyover and an overpass built near Sebastian. More traffic cops were assigned to patrol the streets of Sebastian to further promote tourism because the national government could not slake its thirst for tourist dollars. Another year had passed and a mountain east of Sebastian was stripped of its trees and flattened for the construction of Be Ho Tay's giant mall. In a few months, the first university in Sebastian was erected, the William Howard Taft University.

After a decade, the university released the findings of a study on the two children and 'confirmed' they originated from another planet. The research was authored by Dr. Luisito Magno, a former mechanic who decided to study astronomy after he saw an aurora borealis in his dream. Because of his research work and doctorate from a foreign country, he was appointed as the university's president.

A lot of young people who were the same age as the two missing children had gone on to study at the university. They took up Biology, Physics, Literature, and many other courses. Some of them continued to live in Sebastian and started their businesses. Sebastian's new generation were educated, wealthy; they acted rich, had things enjoyed by the rich, and were rich. They were toe to toe with their counterparts in Manila.

The locals who failed to get into William Howard Taft University remained illiterate, and because there was no way for them to read journalistic sources which were mostly written in English, they could not dissociate themselves from the notion that the kids were born of nature spirits, not extraterrestrials.

It bothered Be Ho Tay that such 'outdated' thinking persisted in Sebastian. To fully win over the masses, he met with the three newsmen again. But the youngest of them had already finished putting his siblings through college and was no longer writing for his paper because, according to his letter to Be Ho Tay, he was not effective as a journalist and was better off as a novelist. At first he refused Be Ho Tay's offer because he could no longer stomach lying, espousing his newfound belief that no servant of arts and letters should engage in duping people through his writing. He also said he wrote about people's universal experiences, not disinformation. But he was no match for Be Ho Tay's powers of persuasion. In exchange for writing propaganda, the Chinese businessman would publish all his works.

Be Ho Tay had a new gimmick. One morning, a strange scene unfolded in front of the Sebastian municipal hall. Three men and a woman were seen wearing shiny metallic clothes and holding bizarre weapons. Anyone trying to stare at the four creatures had to look away from the sharp glare of the sun reflecting off their clothes. "They are space cops," the people whispered among themselves, "and they are after the two missing children who are notorious criminals on another planet." The four 'space cops' suddenly disappeared before experts from the university reached the Sebastian municipal hall. So after ten years, Sebastian was once again in disarray—and this time over 'space cops'.

More and more tourists came to Sebastian. Be Ho Tay became richer than ever. He ended up having five malls, as well as a TV and radio station. He became the mayor of Sebastian, his son a congressman, and his wife the provincial governor. He declared his current mayoral term to be his last one, because he would run as a senator in the next election. He also said that for the national elections he would use Buenaventura, the last name of his 'ancestors'. What he failed to disclose was his need to leverage a name that could be readily enunciated by people throughout the islands. Like his name, Be Ho Tay also changed his religious affinity and became a Catholic to pander to voters in the upcoming national election.

The novelist's conscience continued to rankle him. He struggled with his complicity in the mass disinformation campaign. He knew exactly what he was getting into but could not come to terms with his part in the ludicrous peddling of lies. He did not write, this time, though: he was one of the costumed 'space cops' who pretended to look for the two missing children.

The novelist decided to stay in Sebastian along with his wife and child, and he witnessed first-hand how older people pined for the two children who once brought life to the sleepy town. Some were overwhelmed by their emotions and sobbed helplessly, yearning for a glimpse of those green and black eyes and skin of purest white like the snow from the United States. There was one old man who, until now, was still catatonic from shock; it was widely believed that his soul was taken right after he made eye contact with the green-eyed child. The novelist was deeply moved by this, so he resolved to make amends to the people of Sebastian.

The novelist used his writing to help bring peace of mind to the older residents of Sebastian. He aimed to once again restore truth to a community wracked by greed for money and deceit. And so the novelist wrote. He wrote stories about the two children, sonnets about their love in Sebastian, an epic of their struggles, and a mournful song about their death. According to the novelist, the two children would be alive once again because they were born of the fairies in the Ragasa River.

His writings, however, failed to reach the older generation of Sebastian who could not read. His stories and poems were published by the university and became essential reading materials for literature students. As the novelist grew in prominence, Dr Magno invited him to teach at the university, an offer he immediately accepted. The novelist was thrilled no end, having been given the chance to teach at Sebastian's most prestigious institution.

Be Ho Tay did not waste time fuming over what he perceived was the novelist's treachery. In June, he trotted to Malacañang and asked to buy the town of Sebastian. The president agreed, knowing the national treasury was desperately in need of funds. The president, a womanising drug and gambling addict, was the son of a wealthy socialite. He had no college education and worked as an actor in his youth. He was a famous actor long before he became president.

The sale of Sebastian to Be Ho Tay drove the novelist, on behalf of Sebastian's older residents, into despair. The old folks eventually agreed amongst themselves to go to the Ragasa to plead for help from the two missing children or their parents, who were believed to be nature spirits in the river. None of the elders wanted to be driven away from or forced to be subservient to the all-too-powerful Be Ho Tay—now adopting the name Buenaventura for his political dynasty. They gathered in front of what used to be the Church of St. Francis of Assisi, now a restaurant owned by Buenaventura's son, and then later proceeded to the Ragasa River. Though he kept track of the Ragasa River procession, the novelist was a no-show, preferring to spend time on his short story. "This is another story! This is another story!"

Day and night the elders maintained their vigil on the riverbank. But as soon as the sun was obscured by pale clouds, the old people, weakened by a lack of sleep, groaned from their arthritic and pelvic pain. It was around six in the morning when a scream awakened them. "The children, the children!" exclaimed one woman, who worked selling things at a stall, when she saw the two kids playing in the shallow water on the opposite bank of the river. Everyone couldn't believe what they saw: the children had not aged one bit after over ten years. Many wept in awe as the two children splashed water on each other. The crowd was ecstatic. The only noticeable change in the children was their underwear. They were no longer naked like the time they were first seen in Sebastian.

"I don't care," Buenaventura said when he heard of what had happened. "My transaction with the president will proceed as usual and I will do everything to become a senator in the next election."

The novelist was deeply unsettled by the miraculous reappearance of the once-missing children. His students and fellow teachers noticed his sudden reticence. He left the university one day, went home, headed straight to his room, and didn't come out ever again.

The Buenaventura family became owners of everything in Sebastian. As for the novelist, he was never seen again, which worried his fans. They learned one day about the death of a great man of arts and letters. One night, before dinner, the novelist's wife found him dead on the floor, a spoon lodged inside his mouth. Rumourmongers said it was epilepsy, but the neighbours claimed he accidentally swallowed a spoon as a result of some kind of disability, one that prevented him from writing. But his wife cleared things up. For her, her husband, a great man of arts and letters and Sebastian's greatest writer, swallowed a spoon because he wanted to end his life. ♦

At the Outpost

It was too quiet. A musician with dreadlocks played a djembe, and every note coming off the instrument echoed like the sound of a bouncing ball. Inside the bar, the musician was not the only one who had dreadlocks. If a bomb was dropped on the bar, like that bomb that the Arroyo government dropped on North Cotabato some months ago, that bomb that killed Maguindanaon children in their huts, that bomb that killed all people regardless of their race, religion, gender, and age—Bob Marley would probably die many deaths, and be defaced or have his body parts severed.

But there was no Bob Marley in North Cotabato. He—or his many copycats—was in Cebu City. On the walls of the bar, posters declared March as 'Reggae Month' in Cebu, though they did not mention whether Cebu referred to the entire stretch from Bantayan Island to Oslob, or just to Cebu City alone which did not even extend to Mandaue, or crossed the Mactan Channel to include Lapu-Lapu City.

The posters touted that this was the first 'Reggae Month' in the Philippines. The subtext was that Cebu and not Manila did it first.

Entering the bar, they heard the emcee—who also wore his hair in dreadlocks and was drunk and high on marijuana—proclaim that the night was a Bob Marley Night. All the songs to be played would be Bob Marley songs.

They sat in a corner next to a glass window that looked out to other tables out front, all of which were occupied. The window also showed a view of the bar's front yard, an inclined road used by taxis coming and going from the Marco Polo Hotel as well as cars and motorcycles headed to Busay.

The bar was an old house. From outside, there was no way it could be mistaken for a restaurant because it looked just like any ordinary house for ordinary people—though it was more of a house for drunks these days. To enter the bar, one had to pass through the old balcony bordered by railings. The former parking area next to the house was outfitted with a roof; a canoe was hung overhead and tables placed underneath. Half of the yard, which was likely a garden and a parking space, was also arrayed with tables and chairs; the garden was turned into a parking lot for the bar patrons' cars, SUVs, and motorcycles.

The canoe matched the oars that were used to decorate the interior of the house. But still, it was hard to figure out the main motif of the bar's interior because the wall hangings consisted of photographs which looked as if they were shot somewhere in Central Asia, old electric guitars, and a kudyapi—a native musical instrument that almost spanned the height of an adult person—at the side of the door. Entering the restaurant, Tobias Sto. Niño plucked the guitar strings and realised the instrument was no longer working.

"What do you want to order?" His mouth was close to Sissy Sandoval's ear. The sound blasting from the stage was reaching earsplitting levels. It was accompanied by a chorus of people chanting "Bob Marley!"

"I just need a glass of iced tea," she said, still unable to stop speaking in accented English.

Tobias teetered between annoyance and desire to mock the woman's English. He forced himself to rethink whether it was his Manila sensibility which made him intolerant of Sissy Sandoval's accent or whether there was something truly off and affected about the woman's manner of speaking. Or he was simply annoyed by her pretensions when both of them knew why they had really met up that night.

With his raised right hand, Tobias signalled to a waitress. He asked for a bottle of San Mig Light and a glass of iced tea for Sissy. He was about to order some finger food for her, but caught himself just in time; he estimated his likely expenses for their next stop after this bar.

"I love Bob Marley," Sissy said, to break the silence.

"So I figure. It seems that's the trend here. Almost all the people here look like Bob Marley clones."

"Do you like Bob Marley?"

"I don't do drugs. Do you?" Tobias almost blurted out to Sissy if she could drop her affected English.

"Sometimes," she said, finally in Filipino. "Nothing's wrong with that, right?" Sissy was looking outside at the parking lot.

Say no to authority!
Say no to the police!
We are free!
No to poverty!
No to war! No to violence!
Music and freedom!
Music and freedom!

The DJ did his thing in between the band's performances, shouting out a credo. Tobias couldn't tell whether it was the DJ's way of declaring how drunk and high on marijuana he was or whether he was sincerely calling for those institutions to be demolished. Tobias couldn't decide whether the DJ meant one of the two—or both.

Remove the system!
Destroy the system!
Yes to freedom!
Yes to freedom!

The server finally brought their orders. Tobias watched Sissy's hands closely and how she grasped the iced tea with her right hand, her fingers spread out.

This made Tobias smile, as it reminded him of Sandra Casipe who was, like him, a member of a writers' organisation at the University of Santo Tomas. He met her during a workshop. She was the one who made the first move and introduced herself: "I have this impression that you're easy to be with, you are like a serene mountain." Sandra, a poet, was majoring in literature. In the beginning, they bonded while smoking in a pavilion in front of their school building, chatting, sharing cigarettes, trading jokes. They were in their third year at the time. They became close to the point that he was with her long past midnight while she was writing up her thesis at a Wendy's branch in Dapitan at the back of the university. He also went out drinking with Sandra many times at a carinderia in Maria de Leon, the nearby table occupied by bus drivers and conductors.

"You're easy to be with, *Tomas*," the drunk Sandra always flirted with him this way. "You're like a serene mountain."

It was in these drinking sessions that Tobias noticed Sandra's peculiar way of holding a beer bottle. She curled only three fingers around the neck of the bottle, as if it disgusted her. Tobias kept noticing this as he went out with her in Malate, in Jazz Rhythms, their favourite hangout after class. Sandra indeed seemed to hold beer bottles as if they were dirty. She would carefully place the mouth of the bottle against her lips and slowly swallow her drink, like a sacred and rehearsed ceremony.

Tobias could not forget the last after-midnight dates with Sandra in Jazz Rhythms. The DJ was playing Semisonic's 'Closing Time', a signal to customers that it was the bar's closing time. It was right around December, and Sandra was already drunk. She picked up the tab to celebrate with him about her winning a university writing contest.

"*Tomas*," she whispered, her breath hot against his cheek. "Are you still a virgin?"

He laughed. She asked him again.

"Not anymore," he lied.

Then he could feel her hand on his thigh, her fingers on the zipper of his pants and then on his cock, which slowly stiffened in response to the squeezing motion of Sandra's hand. He felt the warmth of her palm, the tightening hold of her fingers around his cock. His shoulders slightly lifted each time Sandra brushed her pointer against the tip of his penis. He wanted to ask her to stop but the sensation was amazing. Besides, it was dark in that part of the bar and there weren't too many customers at the nearby table. He came in her hands. She wiped his cum against his pants.

"That was fast," she said, gulping her remaining beer; she still held the bottle with her three fingers. "And it's too small..."

"You are disgusting."

They stopped going out after that. Or it was Sandra who kept her distance and never spoke to him again until they graduated. He began noticing her in the company of other poets in their group. Still, he kept seeing her frequent visits to his Friendster account. Maybe she still wanted to check in now and then, perhaps hoping that after ten years, he was still "easy to be with, like a serene mountain".

He smiled before Sissy Sandoval, buoyed by a memory from almost a decade ago.

This was no longer the woman he met earlier at Bo's Coffee inside a Fullybooked branch at Ayala Mall, he thought. Or he might not be the same man as before. He gulped his beer while staring at Sissy, who smiled and nodded pleasantly. Another band was starting to play when Tobias got a hard-on while staring at Sissy and the gaps between her fingers as she wrapped them around the glass of iced tea. This was no longer the same woman he had met earlier that day. This was not the same person who had introduced herself to him at the bookstore.

§

The sun was hot against Tobias's skin but the gusts of wind dampened the heat, so he was comfortable at the balcony of Bo's Coffee along with people who chain-smoked as they bantered and laughed. This coffee shop inside a bookstore was the one place in the buzzing city that he found to be perfect, with people just talking and reading the books they had bought. For three days in Cebu City, Tobias spent all his time either writing in his journal or working on a short story he was rushing for the Palanca Awards in April. His pastimes became writing short stories, reading, and keeping to himself. It was in college at the University of Santo Tomas that he started writing. After he completed his degree in Sociology, he decided to do further study and take up a Creative Writing course. He was unable to return to the university, however, because he had to frequently leave Manila for work.

It was January, and he had just returned from a November relief operation in Pikit, North Cotabato. He spent Christmas and New Year in Davao City, visiting Cebu City before heading home to Manila.

Tobias decided to stay in Cebu City for four days to finish up a report for an NGO he worked for and also to watch the Sinulog festival. Their NGO's advocacy was focused on documenting human rights violations during the military operations in North Cotabato towns. The report was on indiscriminate bombings. In Malacañang, President Arroyo remained tight-lipped because it appeared that public support was on the side of the military operations. Military planes were unstoppable in their carpet-bombing, killing everyone: Moro Islamic Liberation Front rebels, spouses of the rebels, and in September, Moro siblings who were kids. "And now they are going for the rebels' children," he muttered to himself as he wrote his report. Before the New Year, he had already managed to finish half of it, and thus he had some time and decided not to go home to Manila just yet in September.

He wanted a few days off in January and picked Cebu City. "Like Manila, but with mountains and beaches," was how Tobias described it. Because he still had some money left over from his Christmas bonus and 13th-month pay, plus all of his December expenses in Davao City were on a per-diem basis, he could afford booking a four-day stay at the Waterfront Hotel in Lahug. His goal was to watch the Sinulog parade and rest in a city that was not Manila.

As early as December, he had already booked a room at the Waterfront Hotel. During the Sinulog month in Cebu, this was how things went: all hotels were fully booked, plane tickets were snatched up fast, and both ship and plane fares cost almost twice their regular prices. Hence his decision in December to pay for his flight and a room in his favourite hotel. The Waterfront Hotel in Lahug, as well as Montebello near Banilad, were he and his coworkers' favorite destinations whenever they had a conference in Cebu City. Tobias chose the Waterfront Hotel this time because the Sinulog parade was not likely to pass the street along Montebello. This August alone there was another armed conflict in Lanao del Norte and North Cotabato, and a funder in Europe approved further grant extension for their organisation. It would mean more conferences for him to attend in different parts of the country and in Europe, as well as more chances to stay in his favourite hotels in Cebu City.

The Bo's Coffee branch inside the Fullybooked in Ayala Mall became his go-to sanctuary for the four days he was in

Cebu City. He was nearing the end of the short story he was writing, one that he planned to submit to the *Philippines Free Press*. He had drunk three glasses of Numi Tea. As he was on his third glass, Sissy Sandoval arrived.

Tobias was eyeing the building right outside the mall when Sissy sat at the previously unoccupied table in front of the one he was using. Like other Bo's Coffee patrons, she was well-dressed. She had on a black knitted poncho, cream-coloured slacks, flat leather sandals, and a white fitted blouse underneath the poncho, carrying a white canvas shoulder bag. She wore her hair loose, but her pearl earrings were displayed prominently. Until she took out her book, Tobias did not immediately give her his attention as she was dressed in the same way as the Filipino Chinese, Koreans, and call centre agents who hung out in the coffeeshop. He peeked at the cover of the book that she was holding. *The Happiness of Being Alone*. The cover showed a smiling woman, who was likely the author. Tobias figured she got the book from the typical 50-70% discount bin of a bargain bookstore. He went back to his writing.

After almost ten minutes had passed, Tobias noticed that Sissy had moved her chair and oriented it sideways so she was facing the same building along his line of sight. He also caught her surreptitiously glancing at his writing, which he found unnerving.

While reading, Sissy took out her earplugs. And like the bargain-bin book she was holding which did not match her expensive-looking clothes, the wires instantly caught Tobias's attention as they were exactly the cheap ear plug types sold by sidewalk vendors in Philcoa and Baclaran. Or the vendors of Colon. He couldn't describe exactly what he felt was off about her. "If only the earplugs were white, a Nano would have suited her," he whispered to himself.

Sissy Sandoval continued to drag her chair close to his

table until she was sure she had caught his attention. Tobias stopped writing and sighed, a forced and audible sigh to indicate to her the awkwardness of the situation she created.

"What brought you here?" was how she opened up her world to Tobias. In English was how she always started her ritual with strangers in places such as this. Some time ago, she used Tagalog to begin her transactions in Mango, in bars around IT Park that call centre agents frequented. There were times when it became too embarrassing for her, having failed to elicit responses when the person she was trying to chat up was not Tagalog, but a Bisaya, Waray, or Korean whom she mistook for Filipino Chinese. So, from then on, she used English each time.

"I'm here for the Sinulog. And for rest... vacation." It was true that he was in Cebu for the Sinulog and a vacation. And Cebu was also his most favourite destination, as well as that of his coworkers in Manila and his friends. To be sent to Cebu City for a conference was even a 'bonus' for one of his coworkers. Aside from the beaches right outside the city, there were also bars and entertainment halls, as well as women. "Not just the beaches, man," his coworkers in Manila used to tell him. "But the *bitches*. The Bisaya have a hard accent."

It was not only a few times that Tobias had seen proof of his friends' often hyperbolic impressions of Cebu City and its women. Every time he was in Cebu, he made a point to visit the coastal areas, go to the bars in Mango and around IT Park, and get a taste of the women. Sometimes he took the women to the hotel room reserved for him during a conference. But his preferred tactic for these things was to take them either to Queensland or any of the cheap motels along Colon, especially when his per-diem allowance was limited. Sissy Sandoval's approach was not new to Tobias. *All of them were like this*, he thought. *Joiners*. Always on the lookout for men at nearby tables, always smiling. Some wore University of San Carlos uniforms, while some had on typical office worker garb or casual clothes one would associate with people leisurely walking in malls and bars.

"Are you from Manila?" she asked, intruding further into his world.

"Yes. In Pasig. You, are you from here?"

"Ay! No. From Mindanao. Iligan."

§

After the DJ's talk, there were a few minutes of silence as the next band set up their instruments. Tobias gestured for a waiter again. He ordered sisig and a platter of peanuts. He realised that she only drank iced tea when the order arrived. He asked if she wanted alcoholic drinks. She said no, and ordered a mango shake instead. He smiled. She was, indeed, different, unlike the ones he had encountered before during his previous visits to Cebu City.

Sissy knew not to get drunk while working. She could end up drugged or too drunk to have control over her body. She had been doing this for eight years, two years while she was still in high school and six years while in Cebu—what she called her 'sideline', especially when she couldn't find a job. In Cebu, she had engaged in this 'sideline' for six years in between her regular job. She was able to find work in factories in Lapu-Lapu, in Danao. She also worked as a cashier in a bar in Mango, and as a waitress in Banilad. Whenever she lost her job, she went out to find men in the city. In malls, in bars, sometimes in hotel lobbies. The band started up. It was still another Bob Marley song, though the vocalist promised they would play their original composition, which was reggae inspired.

"So, why did you end up in Cebu?"

"Work," she said, in a mix of Tagalog and English.

"My parents are already here. We live in Talamban."

Tobias noticed how she seemed rattled by the food, whether to eat the peanuts or use the spoon for the sisig. He figured she had not eaten lunch yet. He smiled at her.

Sissy Sandoval was still in high school in Iligan City when she discovered this 'sideline'. Envy was her motivation. The same was true for her friends. She remembered Eloisa Cañete, her classmate who always had the latest cellphone and new clothes, arriving in class wearing makeup and perfume. Eloisa was her classmate throughout high school, and they graduated together. In their freshman year, Eloisa was quiet and dressed modestly, the child of a domestic helper in Suarez. No one paid attention to Eloisa. Then everything changed during their third year. It was January.

Classes were suspended for the Christmas break. It was almost three weeks of vacation, but Sissy's family were not in a good place that December. Her father passed away in Marawi. As classes resumed in January, everyone, even their class adviser, was greeted by a brand-new Eloisa Cañete: coloured hair, professionally trimmed eyebrows, makeup and lipstick, and enveloped in an invisible, fragrant cloud of Bench Green Tea cologne. Eloisa, holding a latest-model cellphone, silently took her usual seat in a corner. Her sudden change baffled everyone in the classroom.

After that, Eloisa became famous throughout the campus. She was always seen picking up tabs, with new clothes and electronic gadgets. Her suitors became numerous, as well as the number of people, most of them women, who wanted to befriend her. She had her own groups, her cliques. In those days, Sissy could not stop thinking about Eloisa, about how Eloisa was able to get that much money and how Eloisa could afford those perfumes, new cell phones, and shoes.

Sissy temporarily forgot about her classmates during the Christmas break, when she and her family were busy looking for her father who had disappeared in Marawi. Her strongest memory of her classmates was at the start of classes in June, when the campus was shocked by the arrival of Eloisa and her band of friends, all wearing makeup and perfumed, their eyebrows professionally trimmed, holding their latest-model Nokias. When asked how they were able to afford their pricey wares, they would say: "Just do what Eloisa Cañete does." And then they would giggle.

Just do what Eloisa Cañete does. Sissy Sandoval latched firmly on to these words. But how did one do what Eloisa Cañete does?

Eloisa and her coterie were famous around the campus. Women envied them, and men could not get enough of them. There were nights when Sissy lay sleepless with bitterness towards Eloisa's good fortune. At that time, her mother was in Macau. Whenever she called, Sissy would attempt to divert the conversation into asking for new clothes, shoes, and a Nokia cellphone, but instead they always circled back to her father's disappearance. One time, Sissy could not help herself and asked her mother to send her a bottle of fancy perfume. Her mother responded with nonstop ranting and sobbing. It dawned on Sissy that she could not depend on her mother, who was working as a domestic helper, to have new things and be on the same footing as Eloisa on campus. She had no choice but to approach Eloisa for help.

"All right, in December, you can come with us to CDO," Eloisa said, welcoming her to the group. "Just leave everything to us."

During the December break, they left Iligan for Cagayan de Oro City. And when classes resumed in January, Sissy was already part of Eloisa's in-group. *How easy*, Sissy thought. How easy it was to be part of the group.

By their senior year, they grew bolder and decided to spend their schoolbreak on the 'ultimate travel' and 'level-up challenge'. That meant Cebu, not Cagayan de Oro City or Butuan. Eloisa said that it was easier in Cebu. There were many tourists, foreigners and travellers from Manila. They would earn more than usual in Cebu. And Eloisa was right: Cebu and its neighbouring cities such as Mandaue and Lapu-Lapu did have many fresh opportunities. There were bars, malls, restaurants, beach resorts, and parks. After the schoolbreak, they all returned to class with their brand-new and expensive material possessions. Two of them got American boyfriends who they invited to Iligan for a tour of Tinago Falls.

When they graduated from high school, they also graduated from their 'sideline'. Some of them got married. Some went to college. Eloisa herself went to Manila to stay with her father while she finished college. For Sissy, high school graduation marked the end of her carefree lifestyle and obsession with trends. It also meant her friends were going away. Sissy remained hooked, however, on what made it easy for them to earn money in CDO, Butuan, and Cebu.

When it was confirmed that her father was killed in Marawi—with confirmation not from the police, because everyone in Iligan knew the deadly consequences of challenging a Meranaw in Marawi— Sissy just upped and went to Cebu where the fun never ended, where there was always partying, where there were many foreign tourists and people from Manila. All a clear contrast to Iligan, where there was always violence, especially during Erap Estrada's all-out war with the rebels of Lanao.

§

"Are you bored?" was Sissy's question to the man before her. The band was already singing their original composition, and Tobias yawned. He grinned, ordered three more bottles and asked the waiter for a bucket of ice. Sissy observed him. She looked closely at the face of the man in front of her. He appeared groggy from the alcohol, beads of sweat running down his forehead. She estimated his age to be not older than 30. When their eyes met, she smiled sweetly at him. He placed his hand between her thighs.

"It's the same shit," he said of the band's original composition.

"What do you mean 'it's the same shit'?" She drew her thighs closer against his hand. She wanted him to feel the heat of her pussy. A lot of men had told her that the part between her thighs was particularly warm.

"All their songs... they all sound the same... they all sound like a cheap copy of Marley's song."

And they laughed.

Then grew silent.

"Sorry," Sissy said. "I had no idea this place would turn out this way. It was supposed to be a place for artists. We can go to Kukuk's if you want?" Sissy did choose the place. After Bo's Coffee, she knew the likeliest spot for someone like Tobias. She knew his type like the back of her hand. There were men you took to bars, to Mango, to a mall for a movie, to a beach, to a videoke bar. And there were men like Tobias Sto. Niño: young, loved to read and write, worked for an NGO. She had men like him who worked for NGOs.

"I know Kukuk's place," he told her. "Pretentious place."

She didn't know what to say and was rendered speechless by his groping under the table.

She shifted sideways to convey to him she was not enjoying what he was doing. He slammed his hand angrily against the table. People looked in their direction. Sissy was wide-eyed with fear, recalling the one person she knew who expressed anger in the same way as Tobias. Her father.

§

"He left the house just like that, Ma!" Sissy told her mother who was calling from Macau to ask why her father hadn't been home for three weeks.

"But I told him not to go to Marawi!"

"His coworkers also told him the exact same thing. Papa did not listen."

After a long silence, Sissy heard her mother cry. She set the phone down without saying a word to her.

Sissy's mother was trying to tell her that her father should not have gone to Marawi City, how he most likely had clashed with a Meranaw while he worked in Iligan as a security guard in a factory. The Meranaw he fought with was his shift partner. They traded blows, mouthed threats to each other. The Meranaw security guard did not show up for work again, and some days later, the factory had been shot at by AK-47 rifles. Witnesses described a van stopping in front of the factory, how five men came out of it and started shooting.

A police investigation uncovered the former security guard's role in the ambush, as well as the reason why the company fired him. The details regarding his firing from the factory were mostly unclear, but it was Sissy's father who ratted him out to the management.

Sissy would never forget the number of people who came to their house after that. Friends of their parents tried to persuade his father to leave Iligan for a while until things cooled down. They suggested going to Cebu, to Manila, or to Ilocos, her mother's home province. Her father responded in the same way he expressed anger—by slamming his hand against the table—therefore ending proposed discussions of escape. Three years went by without any untoward incidents. Her father's friends and relatives pressed on and kept reminding him never to go to Marawi.

And yet, her father left one day. He did not say anything. He just upped and left, taking nothing with him, not even a bag. Sissy saw him as he was leaving the house. He even left some lunch money for her two siblings. A week passed, and he had not returned. Relatives looked for him in Cagayan de Oro, Iligan, Linamon, even reaching Kolambogan. One of her father's coworkers said he went to Marawi accompanied by a friend from the factory. As soon as Sissy's mother heard of this, she knew right away what had happened to him.

"Unlike before... how I wish Erap had killed them all," were her mother's parting words the last time they talked on the phone.

It's been eight years since her father disappeared. No news about him, not even a corpse, to give closure. There were rumours about him being seen in Davao, in Manila, in Cebu. But all were unfounded. They accepted the fact that he had been slain. One other thing that really hurt Sissy was her mother's decision not to return to the Philippines. Six months after her father's disappearance, her mother told her she was in a relationship with a fellow Filipino OFW in Macau and they were set to go to Dubai. Sissy's two siblings lived with their aunts, while she made up her mind to go to Cebu.

§

Tobias had already consumed six bottles of beer. It was midnight when the last band finished their set. Sissy felt sleepy. It surprised her why she felt at ease spending time with Tobias. Had she wrapped up this transaction early, she could still join other men. Once again, she watched him. His cheeks had reddened from intoxication, his eyes barely open. His forehead was wide, which made his eyes look more prominent under thick lashes. A handsome man, Sissy thought, which was likely the reason she'd enjoyed being with him for almost half the night.

Tobias got up and headed to the restroom. Sissy, now alone at their table, looked down, pretending to inspect her toes, and avoided the stares of the people around them. She feigned interest in reading text messages on her cellphone. It surprised her, after all this time, that she had never learned to like being left alone at the table by men she had joined. She felt as if the people in the bar were all looking at her. When Tobias returned, he asked if she wanted to leave. He gestured to the waiter about paying the bill.

"But where can we go?" she said.

He scratched his head and said: "Where else but my hotel room."

The two left the bar. As soon as they reached the gate, Tobias hailed a taxi.

In the taxi, both were silent. Sissy looked outside the window. She placed her hand on top of his, smiling at the fact that he did not recoil at her touch. His hand wasn't moving. Sissy knew Tobias could feel the heat of her palm on top of it. It was like holding a hard and old stone that had been petrified for thousands of years.

The taxi stopped in front of the IT Park in Lahug. It idled for a while because of a crash. Traffic on all sides was sluggish. Tobias was visibly annoyed, but the interruption secretly pleased Sissy as it meant she could be with him longer before concluding their transaction in his room at Waterfront. She sighed with relief, a lonely sound escaping with her warm breath.

"What was your name again?" Tobias asked.

"Nini Estrera. You?"

"Tobias," he said, extricating his hand from her hold. He immediately went for the area between her thighs, caressed her crotch covered by her pants. "Tobias Sto. Niño."

Sissy Sandoval smiled, leaning her head against his

shoulder. Both of them stared at the wreck of the two cars that had collided; they were totalled, and looked as if nobody in either one had survived. ♦

Plural

One of these days, Lipoy will find a job. This was what he kept in mind when he left home that Monday. Lipoy was not alone in his daily routine; many other city people started their day by professing their fervent beliefs, too, hoping they would become real. That same Monday, his wife Lita believed the exact same thing. Surely, at some point, her husband would find a job, maybe in construction or a private house. Or perhaps he would cross paths with someone who might ask him to repair something broken in their lives or property. This was, after all, the nature of the city where Lipoy had set out to make his mark: everything depended on the great hand of fate and luck.

Lipoy made sure that before leaving the house, he had everything he could possibly need: hammer, wood chisel, handsaw, smoothing plane, nails. He was unsure, though, of his plan to comb through the city to find his rightful boss. *Ah shit, then so be it!* Lipoy scoffed to himself as he slogged outside their home in Luzon Avenue. Surely, somewhere out there in Manila, something was broken and needed fixing.

"Oy, why don't you just join Maning?" Lita exhorted her husband that morning.

"So Engineer Pantaleon could boss me around? Once I leave—I'm done for good! Putang ina nilang lahat!"

"You and your pride. Do you think it's easy to find a job these days? I can't anymore with your attitude." And Lita slammed the dishes in the sink. Food scraps spilled onto the floor. Morsels slid down the gaps between their coco lumber flooring and landed on Rosalinda's belly in the room below. Rosalinda, wife of Edgar—Lipoy and Lita's de facto eldest child after their firstborn had died—was lying on a sleeping mat, waiting for her husband who worked nights as a security guard at an establishment in Makati.

Lita and Lipoy had nine kids in all; only three of them survived. Their firstborn was abducted during the Martial Law period and was never found, most likely having been killed. Their second children were the twins Nemo and Nema. Nemo was three years old when he caught measles and died; Nema, some months after her twin passed away, died of malnutrition. It was said that Nema was like a bird when she ate tiny pieces of food with her pointer and thumb: a piece of rice, a leaf, a vegetable, a pinch from the body of a slipmouth fish. Lita's other kids also died during childbirth because, as she claimed, they were fathered by a nature spirit, a tikbalang: there used to be a huge acacia tree in front of the couple's house. Lipoy had the tree cut down one day not because a tikbalang had sex with his wife, but because MERALCO paid him to let their electrical wires pass unobstructed across the property. That way, power could be distributed to the neighbourhood up ahead in a subdivision. Lita and Lopoy had a daughter who eloped with a cop who was reassigned in Cotabato City. News reached Luzon Avenue about the cop's death in an ambush, but no update ever came about their prodigal daughter, not about one scrap of her soul. Lita also had a kid who was stabbed by an icepick at a tricycle terminal in Balara.

And Lita had a child killed by a curse. Their son attended a town dance where he met a beautiful girl who agreed to dance with him. And because they were seen exchanging longing glances at each other, someone obsessed with the girl did not like it. One night, while resting inside a mosquito net, Lita's son suddenly had convulsions. He was delirious: his eyes rolled back and his mouth was foaming. Lita called for a folk healer, a herbalist to come over. Incense was lit in front of the house. The herbalist placed matchsticks between the toes of Lita's son—and of course, the herbalist diagnosed the presence of a curse. A powerful sorcerer in Balara had inflicted it.

"Goodness, Apo, what should we do?" Lita said in panic. Lipoy was in Saudi Arabia that time, working as a carpenter in a hospital construction in Jeddah.

The herbalist asked for some leftover rice. As Lita handed over the rice, she noticed the shuffling sounds of lizards in the ceiling. The sorcerer in Balara was becoming more powerful, according to the herbalist who placed the rice on the belly of Lita's son. In the ceiling, the lizards were suddenly quiet. Foam once again gushed from the mouth of Lita's son. He died a few moments later, with bits of rice still adhering to his belly.

That Monday morning, Lipoy rode a bus to Baclaran. He planned to start his job search in Cubao and walk southward to Baclaran. All day, he intended to cover the entire length of EDSA. If he reached Baclaran without finding a job, he would light a candle at the Redemptorist Church and pray that by tomorrow, Tuesday, he and Lita could still find someone to loan them money so he could afford the bus fare to continue his search. Lipoy was already an old man. When he walked, his knees had to take so much strain as if there was a huge rock between his thighs. His hairline was also receding, like the telltale marks of a crown that once indicated youth and time's passage, one that was barely appreciated in old age. His possessions, as well as the tools of his trade, were kept in a green bag with an oversized BOYSEN logo. He wore faded jeans cropped to knee length and a T-shirt with BOYSEN on the breast. It'd been a week since Lipoy started his job hunt, but each day brought nothing but disappointment. Midnight represented an end to a day and its failure; the next morning started with a search for opportunities. This was Lipoy's version of hope.

This was the same hope that informed his life as a construction worker. If his father and grandfather were adept in their use of the hammer, then there was no way he could not learn the skill and pass it on to his children and the grandsons of his grandsons. And surely, his very own Edgar, right after sixth grade, had learned to use the hammer by himself.

Lipoy spent twelve of the 65 years of his life working in foreign countries; he was a construction worker for settlements in rich countries in the Middle East and in many places in Asia. If the universe were based on Lipoy's logic of hope, twelve years was transformative enough: he had finished the concrete lining of their buildings and monuments, installed drains on the rooves of their houses, and cleaned the windows of skycrapers in their cities. He was also able to buy a 21-inch coloured TV, have his remaining daughter finish high school, and build a hut in Bohol for her youngest sister who married a farmer. Lipoy bought all his tools abroad, too: his hammer was from Iraq, the saw from Jeddah, the jack planer from Riyadh, and the chisel from Korea. Lipoy's experience in the construction industry was expansive and had been honed abroad. So it continued to baffle him why he was having a hard time looking for a job despite his mastery of the instruments of his trade.

Lipoy began his journey by riding a bus that would ply the length of EDSA. An ordinary bus, as opposed to an air-conditioned bus, which meant it was a free-for-all of the stink, smoke, and dust of Manila. Ten men immediately rubbed against him as he entered the bus. Some of them pretended to repeatedly switch seats, while the rest tried to rub against Lipoy. The bus reached the palatial Iglesia ni Kristo church in Commonwealth Avenue. Lipoy stayed in his seat, watching the men who tried to get close to him. They appeared to signal to each other silently. In this city, people were too tired to talk, so they resorted to nonverbal communication. The men looked away from Lipoy's questioning gaze and alighted in front of the East Avenue Medical Centre. Lipoy could see some of them grin. As the bus moved again, there was commotion among the passengers hollering out to the men: "A bunch of animals! You are too old not to work decent jobs! Mga kawatan! Kawatan!"

A man tapped Lipoy on the shoulder, and told him: "P're, Mando's gang got you. That's how it is, just luck."

This calmed Lipoy. He reached for his pocket, and surely his wallet was gone. He reached for his bag to check his things to discover that his bag was also gone. There was a tingling in his forehead, and his hands went numb. He inhaled deeply because his chest felt heavy. Then Lipoy sobbed. Some passengers were just looking at him. He drew his legs closer and placed his face against his knees. There was nothing the other passengers could do but give him looks of pity and commiseration, while there were others who grinned while nodding in agreement, as well as others who gave words of comfort and thanks for not being victimised by pickpockets.

By the time the bus reached EDSA, the traffic was close to a standstill, as if the highway was just a huge stretch of parking space. Several passengers who could not deal with the long wait decided to get off the bus and walk all the way to their destination. There was already a large number walking along the side of the highway. The side of the road was a shoreland of people; EDSA highway, on the other hand, resembled a sea of unmoving cars with smoking hoods. Where the sandy shore of people met the sea of cars was a long, frustrating wait and distance to travel.

Lipoy's knees shook when he rose from his seat to get off the bus. Although he knew Lita would be sympathetic to him for the loss of his money and tools, he still struggled with the full extent of the loss, the deep shame he would feel after telling his wife what had happened. "You're here in Manila for a very long time and yet you still get victimised by pickpockets," Lita would likely say but with tenderness and lack of judgment.

His mind was a jumble of thoughts and reflections as he walked the alleys of Cubao-Aurora Boulevard. People coming towards him kept bumping against his shoulders. It was as if they kept avoiding looking him in the eye, or maybe this was only his perception. He clenched his hands and focused on a crowd that was forming. Some people were shouting, their eyes fearful. "My god! That giant could trample us!" one of them said. Lipoy saw passengers quickly alighting from buses stuck in traffic, panic in their faces. A train hurtled by from an overhead platform, and Lipoy saw faces through the windows.

"Maybe it got annoyed and that's why it's rampaging!"

"My goodness, are the Manila Zoo people already here?"

"Putang ina, see how it looks like it has horns!"

"It does look like it can't take the heat. It's not used to being in a tropical country..."

"Imported?"

The size of the elephant rampaging in EDSA-Cubao was almost the height of a two-storey building. When it reached the intersection of EDSA and Aurora Boulevard and blocked the traffic of the two main thoroughfares, vehicles honked at it, which drove the elephant into a frenzy. The train passing overhead made it madder. This elephant was wild and ferocious.

From a distance, it looked like a boulder rolling all about the place. Everything in that part of the city stopped in its tracks. It was scorching hot, and the streets were covered with smoke, soot, and dust. The elephant's skin was slick with sweat. Nobody could see its eyes begging for water, for a gust of comforting cold air in this stiflingly hot place, for an answer to why it was trapped in this fiery, noisy, smoky, dilapidated city.

The melee brought Lipoy out of his reverie, although his mind was still fuzzy. *So what happens now?* He could see the elephant from afar, lashing out in the middle of the street and among the buses, trucks, and skyscrapers.

And he thought of a scene.

The elephant was under a pillar holding up a part of the LRT which was under construction. It was still raging, as if it wanted to flatten whatever was blocking its way. Lipoy walked towards the elephant and faced the large animal. The crowd held their breaths nervously, even those watching inside the buses stuck in traffic. *Who is this old man facing the giant? Is he talking to the elephant? Is he trying to say something about the situation both of them find themselves in?*

The moment Lipoy's eyes met the elephant's eyes, the crowd began to stir. An MRT train went by, and passengers crowded against the window to watch Lipoy's faceoff with the elephant, among them a woman who tried to follow the scene as the train carriage moved away. She thought: *This is the first time I've seen an elephant. It's a good thing I decided to ride an MRT. I wouldn't have caught Alex on time, nor seen an elephant.* She rested her head against the train's glass window, still wearing her oversized black sunglasses. She closed her eyes against the grim scene unfurling below the train. Her eyes had already given her so many glimpses of trouble.

"Oh my god, that poor man!"

"His brains came out!"

"Did you see that?"

"Like a watermelon crushed by a ten-wheeler!"

Terror coursed through Yvonne's body. She imagined how it was to be crushed by that kind of weight, tons of it. The train reached Cubao Station, and a throng of commuters boarded the train. Yvonne was still in her seat. She wore white throughout, from her long-sleeved top and pants to her leather shoes. Even her hair was white. The only touches of colour on her were her red lips and black sunglasses.

Today was the day she would 'catch' Alex in a restaurant they frequented at Greenbelt in Makati. Her boyfriend was not going away or anything, but she needed to get to him on time. Or else they'd end up breaking up. Her time was almost out. She was not literally dying: if what would happen to her in the next three days was considered death, half of her body was actually as good as dead. She was quietly gazing outside. People secretly glanced at her hair because it was already as white as her clothes.

"I need to catch him before it's over," she mumbled to herself. She tightly clutched at the train railing. "This is my last chance."

It was three days ago when Yvonne woke up after a long night being visited by a dream. Like a memory, it was a recurring dream. A recurring dream for six months and she had it almost every night. In her dream, there was a mountain blanketed by snow. White like her hair. She was staring at the mountain, and the mountain was staring back at her smallness. The mountain was muscular and looked as if it had been sculpted, like a man who would repay your love with security, fierce vigilance, and faithfulness to your body. That same morning, she woke up wet between her thighs.

She got up, faced the mirror, and saw the changes in her face, in her eyes. Her pupils were gone. Only the whites of her eyes were left. Fear was not her first emotion. She felt nothing, only curiosity. She did not go blind and could still see things clearly. Tears coursed down her cheeks.

Since then, she wore sunglasses when leaving her apartment. It was noon of the same day when her face turned white, white down her neck to her breasts. Even her nipples had turned white. Her lips, though, remained untouched by the whitening progression.

The next day saw all the hair on her body turn white: her eyelashes, armpit hair, and that between her thighs. Her shoulder-length curly hair looked like uncooked sotanghon noodles placed on her head.

"Why is this happening to me?" Yvonne did not know who else to ask about the changing of her body. For two days, she skipped her classes at the university. She very much wanted to call her mother, a domestic helper in Hong Kong, but could not bring herself to unload on her and give her more worries. She had no friends at the university. Alex was the only person she could talk to, but he was in the office and didn't want to take her calls at work since his coworkers didn't know about their relationship. Alex's wife used to be his coworker. Plus, Alex didn't want to be interrupted when at work.

"Alex?"

"Why are you calling? I told you I'd text you first before you can call. I am busy!"

"I know. It won't take very long. I need to talk to you. This is important."

"Important?"

"Something's happening to me?"

"Again?"

"No. This is not about me wanting us to cool off."

"So, what is it this time? I don't want another of those freaky stories about Mt. Everest in your recurring dream."

She did not know what to say next.

"Why are you crying, Yvonne?"

"Something is happening to my body. Let's meet up, please... tomorrow morning. Same place."

"Shit! Are you pregnant?"

"No."

"Okay. Is this cancer?"

"No!"

"Are you okay, Yvonne?"

"Tomorrow. Nine a.m. At Café Breton."

That night, she dreamed about the mountain again. She was staring at the mountain and trying to make out its peak. Chilly and dense air blew against her face. In the dream, her hair was still black and her skin brown. From a distance, a man walked towards her. He drew nearer and nearer. She couldn't wait and rushed to meet him. Lustful desire goaded her to see the approaching man.

"How have you been, Yvonne?"

"You know me?"

"Of course. There were many of us at the mountaintop, all looking at you. We've been waving to you for a long time to get you to climb, but it seems you can't see us."

"There are still people on the mountain?"

"There's a lot of us out there. We keep waving to you to climb, but you keep standing here."

"Sorry, I can't see you. The snow has covered everything."

The man turned to look at the mountain and grinned. "Not true. I can see them from here. There, see how the mountain is filled with people!"

Yvonne saw nothing of the sort. This made her sad and she had to turn her back on the man. She cried and cried until she felt his embrace.

As soon as she woke up, on the third day, she got dressed quickly to see Alex. That was also when she realised her time was running out. In the bathroom she noticed a hole in her white breast. The hole was as big as a basketball and went all the way to her back. Her body was intact, though, because she could still feel and touch her skin over the hole. It was just that she was slowly disappearing. It made her giggle to see her other breast in the mirror; only half of her left breast had disappeared.

"I need to move fast before I become completely invisible. I want Alex to see me before I get eaten away by invisibility. At least someone can attest that I once lived... and continue to live even if others can't see me."

She got off at Ayala Station and brisk-walked along the malls to Café Breton in Greenbelt. In her haste she failed to notice that her clothes were slowly falling off. She was passing in front of the beautiful fountain outside Café Breton when she realised it was already too late. She had totally disappeared, although she could still hear her breathing, touch herself, and see everything around her. She sat at the side of the fountain in the middle of the lavishly appointed place. And she watched Alex. How he waited for her. This was the first time he had to wait for her. Whenever they had meetups, it was always her who did all the waiting. Alex was not a patient man. He left five minutes after nine.

Yvonne didn't know that she was not actually thoroughly invisible. Some people had it in them to see her. From his seat, Edgar could see her. Edgar, Lipoy's eldest son, was on his way home after working the nightshift at a bar on the third floor of Greenbelt. He could see Yvonne's stark-naked form. Edgar stopped walking and could not believe his eyes. He thought that his lack of sleep and exhaustion were making him hallucinate this scene. No, a naked woman sat at the side of the fountain.

The fact that no one else reacted to the naked woman baffled Edgar. Even the security guard at the doorway of Café Breton was unbothered. The thought of having seen a ghost filled him with dread, but he ultimately decided to go down to the floor area where the naked woman sat next to the fountain.

Yvonne, who left as Edgar was finding his way down to the mall's lower level, was no longer at the fountain area when Edgar got there. Yvonne went to the Chapel to pray because of what she had been meaning to do next: to got to the top of the tallest building in Makati to kill herself.

She figured no street sweepers would have to deal with the bloody mess she would make, no pedestrians would be hassled by her splattered body parts on the asphalt, no cops and reporters would need to bother with her death. With the certainty that everything would remain ordinary, including the daily rush hour in the streets of her city, she decided to kill herself.

"I was sure I saw a naked woman at the fountain," Edgar whispered to himself as he rode a bus home. He was still wrapped up in disbelief. "But no way the people around wouldn't react to a naked woman in their midst. The security guards wouldn't allow it, either." He had so many questions. These past few days alone had brought him many unexplainable happenings whose meanings he could not decode.

It had been two days since he kept seeing his father as a headless figure whenever the latter used the mirror to check himself. Lipoy didn't appear to be bothered by this as he continued to comb his hair. Edgar wanted to approach his father about it but was constantly dissuaded by his belief that if he mentioned it to Lipoy, the premonition might come true. Truth remained a vicious thing, though Edgar believed he always had a choice whether to allow it to stay and live in his world.

The bus Edgar was on was stuck on the EDSA and Ayala routes. He could not get the strange sight at the fountain out of his mind. "Who was that naked woman? Was she real or just my hallucination? Putang ina..." He rested his head against the glass window and looked outside the bus. He never rode the train to get home from work; it was always the bus since he started working in Makati. He could rest during a bus ride, could reflect on the things he hadn't given much attention to, and see the world as if viewing the entirety of a parade from a stationary location. It was also during a bus ride that he had a chance to talk to himself.

His mother said he was 'different' compared to his siblings, though he did not ask what she meant by 'different'. As far as Edgar was concerned, his relationship with his parents wasn't that deep. He couldn't remember a time when he was able to confide about what angered him, or made him feel any strong emotion, to his mother.

Once he heard them talk about him.

"Your son is always lost in his thoughts."

"I don't know what's up with you, Lita, stop with that nonsense. He's just not the outgoing type. That doesn't mean he's always lost in his thoughts."

"Sometimes, I really can't understand your son. Sometimes, he scares me... of what he is going to say that maybe... I might not understand or he'll say something that's hard for me to accept..."

"What? I don't know, Lita, you're not making sense."

"I'm telling you, your son scares me..."

Since then, Edgar distanced himself from his mother. He could not understand why he didn't feel comfortable around his mother. There were times their interactions became awkward, as if they were two strangers who did not know each other. *So that's what happens when you discover someone is scared of you... a gap between you is formed*, was how he rationalised to himself what was happening.

The bus stopped at SM Megamall. Edgar looked at the giant billboards attached to the mall's tall, wide building. *Beautiful creatures, beautiful sight*, he would tell himself at the sight of the fashion models on the billboards.

"But what is beauty?" a man next to him asked. The man was older, wearing a nicely tailored polo and holding a briefcase.

Edgar was speechless but it seemed the man could read his questioning eyes.

"You said 'beautiful creatures, beautiful sight' at the

pictures at Megamall. Now I'm asking you, what is beauty?"

This frightened Edgar. "Wait, I didn't say such a thing!"

"You did not say it but you were thinking it."

"Can you read my mind?" Edgar wanted to stand up and sit elsewhere as the encounter was quickly creeping him out. How could this man possibly know what he was thinking?

"Don't worry, Edgar. I am not an evil person. I'm just a poet."

"If you're not evil, then how come... how come I can't hide anything from you?"

"You really can't hide anything from me. And because of that, I can't possibly be evil. If I were evil, then there would be things about you that I would not know. For example, your mother, father, your siblings, even your wife."

Edgar bowed his head, his nervousness causing him to sweat.

"You're the one who's evil, Edgar. You assign motives to people because of how they see you. You never open yourself up to them in the first place. This morning, you caught a glimpse of something in this world... in your place of work, right?"

"Caught a glimpse? I have no idea what you're saying. Never mind."

"You saw life's nakedness. Someone showed herself to you. That's courage."

Edgar quickly thought of the woman next to the fountain at Greenbelt. "That's right. It was her... it was her."

The man got up and told the conductor he was getting off the bus. Edgar was left with so many questions. The man did not even look back to spare him one last glimpse. Edgar sank further into his seat, watching the people outside the bus waiting for all sorts of things, the houses and buildings along the side of the road. Every day he passed that route, and every day the city changed its appearance. His right hand felt numb. He could not move it. This usually happened whenever he was emotionally strained, by anything from anger and fear to unrequited love. How was it possible that someone could read his thoughts? How could he hide himself from this world now, if a stranger could just as easily see into the deepest parts of his being? He was in a mental haze from the time he got off the bus for his entire walk home.

"Another tiring work day, Edgar?" Lita greeted him as he entered the house.

He paused and looked at his mother. They eyed each other for a long time. Edgar bowed his head and retired to his room. Lita was left standing, confused. Then she broke down and cried. She could no longer recognise the person she had given birth to. Her muffled sobbing became a mournful wail.

From his bed, Edgar could still hear his mother. He closed his eyes, and thought about how, later, when his father Lipoy got home, he would tell his parents that he wanted to die. He wanted to end hoping for an opportunity that would never come.

What Edgar did not know was that, in the city where he was placed, decision-making was in the hands of fate. ♦